SPIDERS FROM MARS

SYLVIA STRYKER
SPACE CASE #4

SPIDERS
FROM
MARS

DIANE VALLERE

Polyester Press

LOS ANGELES | READING

SPIDERS FROM MARS

Sylvia Stryker Novel #4

A Polyester Press Publication

Print ISBN: 9781939197818

eBook ISBN: 9781939197825

To Ziggy Stardust and the Spiders from Mars

OPERATION NEPTUNE'S DEAD
EXTRACTION LOGS: SUSPECTS,
ACCOMPLICES, AND PERSONS
WITH UNKNOWN MOTIVATION

*(Results of Preliminary Background Check,
compiled by Lt. Sylvia Stryker)*

Anderson, Angie: Former pop singer turned uniform company owner. Sylvia's boss at Century 21 Uniforms.

Bolder: SPIDER.

Cat: Sylvia's self-built robot cat. Performs various computer functions in addition to acting like a cat.

Champion, Zeke: Son of spaceship repairman. Expert on hacking and space drone technology.

Corsair, Cosmos: Space pirate locked up in Federation Council prison. Synthesized and distributed HAx5, a hallucinogenic drug that led to an epidemic throughout the galaxy.

Doc Edison: Head of Medi-Bay.

Forari, Lita: Laundress at Federation Council prison.

Garson: Prisoner at Federation Council prison.

Marshall, Vaan: Youngest member of Federation Council. Sylvia's first love. Plunian.

Neptune: Head of security for Moon Unit Corporation. Large, intimidating dude. Currently serving time in Federation Council prison for a crime he did not commit.

Pika: Pink Gremlon girl alien. Possible troublemaker.

Ronson: SPIDER.

Space Pirates: Bad dudes who do bad things.

Stardust Cowboys: Independent security team hired to work Moon Unit: Mars.

Starr, Ofra: Engineer of Moon Unit 6. Preference for glittery eyeshadow. Recently came into vast wealth and now is part owner of Moon Unit Corporation.

Stryker, Sylvia: Space Academy dropout. Half Plunian and half human. Has lavender skin.

Grew up on a dry ice farm. Difficulty breathing unregulated air without a bubble helmet. Acting uniform lieutenant for Moon Unit Corporation. Part-time sales rep for Century 21 Uniforms. Lead operative in Operation Neptune's Dead. Basically, the brains behind the operation.

Tom, Captain Major: Commanding officer of the Moon Unit 8. Former naval captain. Makes frequent reports to ground control.

Tulsa: Employee at Federation Bureau of Affairs.

Woody: SPIDER.

1: CHANGES

THE FIRST THING I DID WAS HAVE NEPTUNE declared legally dead. It was an unlikely start to a rescue mission, but it was my first one, and Neptune's incarceration made it difficult to ask him for advice.

Neptune, of course, wasn't dead. He was serving time in a minimum-security prison on Colony 1 after helping me hijack a privately owned spaceship. It was all in a day's work for high-level security agents like us, but to the Federation Council, it was a violation of law, and somebody had to pay.

Okay, fine, *Neptune* is a high-level security agent. *I'm* a lieutenant for an outer-space cruise ship. But I trained to be a security agent before a whole lot of crap changed the course of my life, and when Neptune gets out, I'm going to hit him up with a proposal he won't be able to turn down. Partners. The best-dressed security team in the galaxy.

(Not that Neptune cares all that much about uniforms, but I figure I should play to my strengths.)

But that's later, and this is now. Neptune's been in prison for the past four months, and no doubt anything I say now you'll miss because you'll be comparing "the first thing I did" with "four months" and asking yourself, "Geez, Sylvia. The man is in prison. What took you so long?"

I'll tell you what took me so long. No matter how many intergalactic libraries you hack into, you'll be hard-pressed to find an article titled "Tips for Busting Your Mentor Out of Jail."

What you *will* find are stories of corruption. Of people locked up for crimes they claim they haven't committed. Stories about prisoner abuse, confessions from inmates on their death beds, and if you're lucky, when your eyes are blurry in the middle of the night after weeks of combing through the *Galaxy News* archives, you'll find an interview by a former warden with the information you need.

If you have any ideas about breaking someone out of jail, forget it. It's far easier to get a dead body out of prison than a live one.

That's where I got the idea.

Drafting a prison break is easy-peasy once you have step one. I had step one. I didn't waste time studying the language needed to write a suitable legal notice. I hacked an example from the local mortuary database, forged a signature, and filled in the blanks like a Mad Libs game. I carried my paperwork on board Moon Unit: Mars, the cruise ship where I work as the uniform manager, and kept it under my pillow until today, when a twenty-four-hour layover left me a window to file it at Federation Bureau of Affairs before continuing our journey. See? Easy-peasy.

In the past, a Moon Unit would leave the space station and fly directly to our destination. Planets farther away required a combination of thrusters, propellant, wormholes, and gravity assists to get to their destinations. That created an environment where anyone on a Moon Unit couldn't get off a Moon Unit until it got to where it was going, which would be fine under normal circumstances but not so much when there's a murderer on board the ship. (You might think that's an odd extreme, but the outer-space cruise industry is relatively new and unregulated, and a surprising number of incidents involving murder and cruises illustrated a hole in the legislation that defines such things.)

After more than one such situation, Federation Council, started requiring all passenger-carrying ships to stop at Colony 1. The idea was to receive an inspection and clearance before embarking to be sure there were no side missions on anybody's agenda.

Colony 1 was where the Federation Council congress was located. It was also where politicians, rich folks who did bad things, and temporarily detained convicts were incarcerated. It was where Neptune had been taken after his arrest on Saturn, and after hacking into the prison system, I'd confirmed there were no plans to move him anytime soon.

It was a warm day. Temperatures lingered over eighty degrees. The dry climate, combined with a uniform that regulated my body temperature, made it bearable. The uniform in question was a white Stealthyester® jumpsuit with blue trim. It covered everything but my head, which was protected by a bubble helmet that ensured I got breathable air.

Lines of people filled the interior of the

Federation Bureau of Affairs. Nobody actually liked making trips to the agency, but certain actions required the effort. I doubted my supervisors at the Moon Unit Corporation expected me to spend my day off filing paperwork, but that was just as well. While other members enjoyed the local tourist attractions, I had a window of relative anonymity to complete my covert business.

A person with less to lose would look for the shortest line or the most efficient teller. I looked for the least threatening. The teller at the last window on the end was a petite, girl with a sweet disposition. She wore blue lipstick that matched her blue hair, both of which made her standard Federation uniform appear trendy. Her line was several people deep, but for what I was about to do, I considered her an easier mark than the curmudgeons behind windows three, four, and five. (Window six had a sign that said, "On Break.)

For the next twenty minutes, the room was filled with little more than, "I'll be assisting you today," which must have been the tellers' version of "May I help you?" in a department store. The responses were either inaudible or ridiculously boring. After four missing person cases, a name change, and a requisition for early retirement payment, I tuned them out.

Eventually, I reached the front of the line. "Name?" the blue-haired young woman asked.

"Sylvia Stryker."

"I'm Tulsa. I'll be assisting you today." She pushed her blue bangs away from her forehead. "If I get hit on by one more guy pretending to file a missing person report for his ex-girlfriend, I'm going to start wearing a fake wedding band." She grinned. "Whatcha got?"

"Death notification." I passed my signed (forged) and notarized (official) (-ish) documents under the phaser-proof glass while the woman checked my credentials. She held my ID card over a scanner and turned her head away while a bright light pulsed underneath the surface. She handed the ID card back, glanced over my paperwork, and made a sympathetic sound.

"Your friend had quite an accident," Tulsa said.

It hadn't been easy to come up with a plausible method for Neptune to have died while in prison, and I'd discounted any of the more gruesome ways so I wouldn't have nightmares picturing them. Reality dictated that I needed some details to sell the fib, so I fabricated a story involving his trademark military attire and a cargo-net malfunction.

"It's sad. If only he'd been wearing his regulation uniform, none of this would have happened." (Neptune never did give my job as uniform manager the proper respect.)

Tulsa smiled what I guessed was one of many pitiful looks she passed off during the day. I studied her face—mouth turned down, blue lips pursed, chin dropped—and thought about how often I'd seen that expression in my life. I learned at an early age that people were generous when it came to pity, but pity didn't pay the bills. Sometimes, when the circumstances were right, lying, cheating, and bartering did. (Pity helped make it easier to fool people, though, so it wasn't a hundred percent unwelcome.)

Tulsa's expression changed from pitying to judgmental. "You're taking his death very well," she said suspiciously.

Yes. Right. I inhaled deeply, exhaled, and pretended to choke back tears before raising my eyes to meet hers. "It hasn't been easy," I said. "When I first heard, I lost my mind. I couldn't function." I glanced to either side and dropped my voice. "My doctor prescribed an antianxiety drug to help me cope. I probably shouldn't still be taking it after four months, but it hurts so much, knowing he's gone."

"I didn't know. I'm sorry." She stretched her hand out from behind the phaser-proof glass and tapped the back of mine. A small blue lightning bolt that matched her hair and lipstick was tattooed on the back of her wrist. "You'll get over him in time," she said. "When my husband died, I was on medication for a year. It got so bad, I—" She seemed to realize she was on the verge of confessing deep, dark secrets to a stranger, and she cut herself off. "If you need help getting off the medication, let me know. I entered a recovery program on Mars. It was effective until—well, if you need assistance, I can help you find it."

I forced a smile and squeezed the tips of her fingers in solidarity. Truth? I wasn't on any drug. I was on a mission, and that meant every person I encountered was either an enemy or an ally. I learned that at Space Academy before dropping out, and experience had only illustrated the lesson in real time.

Most people go through life exchanging pleasantries and being polite, never stopping to listen to what others are saying. This isn't one of those learn-to-listen lectures that promises you can improve your marriage or gain trust from your employees. It's a fact: Let people tell you more than you ask. File it all away for later. You never know what you'll need when you initiate a mission. The only thing you can control is knowing who to go to when you come up against something unexpected.

I finished at the window. Now to wait out the natural news cycle. In the next couple of minutes, my paperwork would be fed into a scanner. Words would be extracted, plugged into a news template, and dumped into a database of stories. At the same time the stories were streamed onto computer screens, they would appear on a marquee that wrapped around the perimeter of Federation Council. Somewhere between "Space Pirate Sabotage on Saturn" and "Vandalism on Venus" would be Neptune's death: "Blacklisted Commander Turned Security Expert Deceased After Cargo-Net Accident in Prison Storage Unit."

Once the information found its way into the prison computers, Neptune's name and history would be extinguished. It would be as though he spontaneously combusted. If Neptune had made friends on the inside, they might be a complication, but Neptune wasn't the friend-making type. I guess that's why loners are loners; they like the simple life.

I wasn't without experience when it came to arrest protocol. When my dad was arrested, the news traveled so fast our dry ice farm went from being a respected supplier to a wasteland of rubbish almost overnight. We were social pariahs. After the council threatened to shut us down, we were left with a fate even worse: invisibility.

If I could render Neptune invisible inside the prison, I'd have a shot at getting him out.

A steady stream of visitors flowed to and from the building. Efforts had been made to make the air and surface quality of Colony 1 hospitable to the largest majority of those visitors, and in addition to the synthetic oxygen mix that a local team of chemists had developed and sold to the government, there were gravity bars where people congregated and shops to fulfill travel and tchotchke needs. Culinary spots had popped up, too, and now a visit to Colony 1 could net you the best cup of coffee in the universe.

On principle, I drank tea.

The courtyard outside Federation Bureau of Affairs was active. Vendors with small carts sold snacks to employees on break and visitors who'd made the trip for personal reasons. I peeled off the lid to my hot tea and people-watched, letting the beverage cool. It wasn't that people-watching was entertaining. It was training. Most people existed in their own worlds, unaware of what their actions and outfits said about them. I considered this an ongoing part of my security training, being able to assess a crowd, identify threats and allies, and build character profiles based purely on observation. It wasn't a lesson I learned from my security training education or from Neptune during the short time he tutored me. I came up with this one myself.

I tested the air quality with my portable molecule tester and, when the reading came back with a positive result, removed my helmet and set it on the bench next to me. I blew on the surface of my tea and then sipped. The beverage was flavored with a hint of zinnia, the most prevalent flower in outer space, leaving behind a lingering sweet note to counter the bitter bite of the tea. I swirled it around over my tongue then swallowed, closing my eyes while the hot liquid slid down the back of my throat. It wasn't usual for me to indulge in the cost of a cup of brewed tea, but it also wasn't usual for me to spend my day at Federation Bureau of Affairs having someone declared dead. It seemed this was as good a time as any to try to blend in and act like everybody else.

The news banner around Federation Council Headquarters blinked three times in rapid succession, indicating a reboot of the system. This would be followed up with updated news stories and crime reports. The system was automated after Tulsa fed my forms into the computer but depended largely on the reports ahead of it. I was tense, needing to see the news of Neptune's demise proclaimed to the world before counting my mission as complete.

The banner of news started streaming. "Record-Breaking Temperatures Expected on Mars" * * * "Federation Council Vote on Proposed Law Changes in Next Twenty-Four Hours" * * * "Drug Epidemic Reaches Dangerous Levels" * * * "Prisoner Murdered while Serving Life Sentence" * * * "Animal Shelters Reach Peak Capacity" * * *

The tension within me ratcheted up. Prisoner murdered while serving a life sentence? That wasn't right.

I sat my tea on the bench and checked my documents on my portable device. The language was clear. Neptune died while unloading cargo from storage. A regulation uniform could have saved his life. It was an unfortunate accident that could have been avoided.

No mention of murder. No mention of anything suspicious. I'd purposely kept it as bland as possible to not attract attention.

Murder attracted attention.

The word "murder" was charged with everything I wanted to avoid. A freak accident could happen. It could be brushed under the rug. It wouldn't cause anybody to do anything differently. But a murder propelled all sorts of people into action, and a report of a murder would certainly lead to a body that was very much alive.

I stood and juggled my helmet, my cup of tea, and my portable document device. The tea fell and splattered by the toe of my boots. Someone called out my name and I shielded my eyes and searched for the source.

"Sylvia! Over here!"

I zeroed in on the source. It was Tulsa, the teller from Federation Bureau of Affairs. She was shorter than she'd appeared when she filed my paperwork. She came at me so fast her blue hair blew away from her face. "I was hoping you were still here," she said. She put one hand on her side and bent toward it. "Side stich. Ow."

I pointed at the streaming news banner. "There's a mistake—"

"No mistake," she said. She straightened and grabbed my arm. "Come with me."

I followed her behind the building to a small garden. The rocky surface area of the colony had been carved away, and small succulents that survived in dry climates covered the ground. There was no way they'd grow on their own, and I wasted a brief thought condemning the council for wasting resources on the beautification of their property and not improving the quality of life for residents under their government.

"There was a problem with your paperwork," Tulsa said. "It was rejected from the system because of duplicitous intel."

"There's a mistake. Neptune wasn't murdered. He was in an accident. An *accident*," I repeated.

"It's no mistake," Tulsa said. "Check your device."

I tapped the screen and swiped through pages of reports that had been filed that morning. My report wasn't there, but the headline I'd seen streaming around the perimeter of Federation Council was. "Prisoner Murdered While Serving Life Sentence" read the headline. Underneath, in the body of the report, were the details, and that's when I knew my plan to break Neptune out had gotten complicated exponentially.

The murder victim wasn't Neptune.

The suspect was.

2: CONFLICT REPORT

There was one surefire way for Neptune to screw up my plan to have him declared dead, and that was to be the lead suspect in an ongoing murder investigation. No way would the staff inside the prison take their eyes off him now.

"The computer extracted enough words from your paperwork to initiate a conflict report," Tulsa said.

I stared at her. "What's a conflict report?"

"When two reports are filed and the system recognizes similar information, they're compared to verify sources and make sure the same report doesn't get filed twice. Your report triggered the comparison, but there were too many differences. You said Neptune was dead. The original report says Neptune committed murder. Those two things can't exist at the same time."

"How does the system know which report is real?"

"It doesn't at first." She chewed her lower lip. Her blue lipstick had worn off in patches, and her front teeth were stained with it. Her eyes were wide and round, orbs tinted purple, lined with long, curled black lashes. When I first encountered her in the line, she looked stylishly cute, but in the past hour, she'd lost her quirky vibe. "As soon as I saw the alert, I tried to reject your documents, but they'd already been filed. I rebooted the system to make it look like a computer malfunction."

"Does that happen often?"

"It's a computer. It doesn't make mistakes."

"Can you talk me through how the system works?"

She glanced over her shoulder at the building. "I don't have a lot of time now," she said. "They think I'm on my break. But it's like this: when a conflict report is triggered, the computers generate intel for an investigation. If the internal investigators can't quickly explain the conflict, I'll be called in for an inquiry."

"Then what?"

"I don't know. I've never been in on an inquiry. I can't tell you what's going to happen after that."

A small device on her wrist lit up and blinked. "I'm out of time. I have to get back." She turned around and fled, leaving me alone among the succulents.

This was possibly very not good.

The tension I felt while sitting in the courtyard hadn't left me, and now a buzzing sensation filled my chest, arms, and legs. I knew the air quality was safe, but I snapped my helmet on and released a booster of oxygen to calm me down.

If I'd taken advantage of Federation Council's emergency response offer of housing for all Plunians after our planet was blown up, I'd be close enough to home to stop by for a much-needed break. But Federation Council, while publicly describing themselves as fair government for the galaxy, had privately screwed me over one too many times. After stealing a Moon Unit with Neptune, solving the murder of a space courier, and saving a race of aliens from total annihilation, I figured I'd earned my independence.

I moved into Neptune's house (he wasn't using it). I emptied out his garage and made it my home. I may have sold off a few things to raise capital for my rescue mission, but it wasn't like Neptune was using them either.

My space pod was parked in a visitor lot on the east side of the Federation Council Park, and I was tempted to go straight to it and leave. I had no idea what would happen when the inquiry into my news item hit the desk of Federation officials, and a part of me—the part that didn't trust elected officials—thought it prudent to be as far away from Federation Council as possible when that happened. But there was another part of me that knew Neptune was inside those prison walls. And he was now suspected of murder.

Whatever had happened was still unknown. What I did know was this: the Federation Council Penitentiary where Neptune was serving time was a minimum-security prison. It was where those who'd served in the military went, a concession to the good they'd done before turning bad. Neptune's incarceration was a technicality that could have been avoided if members of government weren't such blind rule followers, and I'd actually believed that they were locking him up for show with the plans to release him when news of his (our) crime died down. They didn't.

But if Neptune were convicted of murder, then

everything would change. He'd lose any perks he had from serving in the military. There would be no parole, no prisoner rights, no chance at freedom.

Neptune would know all this. If an inmate had been murdered, then someone else committed the crime. It was no longer my job to have him declared dead. It was my job to have him found innocent of a crime he didn't commit.

I hoped. Because if Neptune *did* commit the crime, my job of rescuing him was about to get a whole lot more difficult. As much as I wanted to leave, I couldn't. Not before finding out what had happened behind those prison walls.

Tulsa hadn't shared details of the murder, and I regretted not focusing on my need to know more when she was standing in front of me. My choices for intel were limited, but there was one option. I knew someone in Federation Council, someone I had mixed feelings about seeing again. It was time to pay my ex-boyfriend a visit.

Vaan Marshall was the youngest member of Federation Council. Of the twenty-three members of the council, he was the only one who hadn't been born into a legacy position. He achieved his rank the hard way: through high grades and networking. After graduating from Space Academy with honors, he'd been the top choice to inherit a position vacated by a council member with no family to carry on for him.

Vaan and I had dated through much of our time together at the academy. He was Plunian—*all* Plunian—which gave him a vibrant purple color that contrasted greatly with his bright-green eyes. He had no hair, which simplified his morning routine in addition to giving him an air of confidence and sex appeal that men burdened with hair lacked. Vaan had extended an anytime-you-want invitation to me after the last time we saw each other, and if he hadn't been responsible for having Neptune arrested, I might have taken him up on the offer. But for as close as Vaan and I had once been, we too often found ourselves on opposite ends of the universal code of right and wrong. He followed the rules, and I did what I thought was right. You might think those two were the same thing, but you'd be wrong.

Federation Council offices were the tallest of the quad, behind the administrative buildings. I left my helmet in place (it was more convenient than carrying it) and followed the trails through the manicured gardens to the entrance. After giving my name and completing an ocular scan at security (standard protocol for government buildings other than the FBA), I was escorted to Vaan's office by a white robot built like a refrigerator.

"Syl-vee-ah Stri-i-i-i-i-i—" The robot got caught on my last name and stuttered on an indefinite loop.

"Robot, reset!" said a voice behind me. I turned and saw a skinny, pale-pink alien girl grinning broadly.

"Pika?" I asked.

"It's meeeeeeeeeeeeeee!" she cried. She opened her arms wide and threw them around me, a hug that felt more like pipe cleaners than arms. I hugged her back gently but with genuine affection.

Pika was a Gremlon. They were the silliest aliens in the galaxy and were hard-pressed to find and hold down real jobs. On a recent trip to Saturn, Pika and her fellow Gremlons had gotten into some trouble that turned out far better than it might have, thanks to yours truly. The downside to a species of innocent aliens being in a life-threatening situation that involved murder was that some of that innocence had been lost. Pika, who'd formerly existed as a stowaway who caused more problems than she solved, had accepted work at the council as Vaan's personal assistant.

The last time I saw Pika was the day Neptune had been arrested. Unlike me, who had watched the whole thing go down, she (and her fellow Gremlons) had been placed under the care of Vaan, moved to the Federation Council for a debriefing and posttraumatic stress analysis. I knew then that Pika had been fascinated with Vaan, so when I heard he'd given her a job, I found it sweet. I doubted she got much done, but the entertainment factor surely was worth it.

When she released me from her spindly hug, she stood back and grinned. Her mouth, filled with fifty-two teeth, stretched from ear to ear. I stepped backward like I always did in the face of so much enthusiasm.

It was easy to lose time while talking to Pika. The months that had passed between the last time I saw her and now would be filled with stories she'd like to share, but time wasn't on my side. "Is Vaan in?" I asked. "I need to talk to him. It's important."

Pika's smile shrank a bit. The word "important" was a trigger for someone like her, who took most things lightly and expected no consequences to her actions. To put Gremlons to work in any capacity meant they'd have to be mentally retrained to respond to certain commands in a Pavlovian manner.

"Vaan isn't here anymore. He left in a hurry this morning after scanning the daily news bulletins."

I felt a chill run up my spine. It was natural for Plunians to run hotter than everybody else, but the chill had nothing to do with my physiology. "Did he say where he went?"

"To the prison," Pika answered. "He said something happened this morning and he had to take care of it before things got out of hand."

3: VAAN MARSHALL

THE SHIVER OF ANXIETY ESCALATED. MY BODY temperature rose, but I felt cold at the same time. "Did Vaan say anything else?"

"No," Pika said in her soft, squeaky voice. The smile was completely gone from her face, and her mouth turned down slightly at the sides. "I came in early so I could go to the prison, but I needed Vaan to sign off on my visitor pass first. I told him I wanted to go see the spiders, but Vaan said no."

My first thought was to ask about the spiders, but Pika often went off on tangents. It wasn't beyond her to befriend actual spiders, though I suspected her conversations with arachnids would be amusingly one-sided for anyone not afraid of them.

"Vaan said no?" I prompted. It was good to keep Pika on track.

"He asked me to hold on while he finished approving the news bulletins, and then he turned bright purple, and then he left in a hurry."

"Did he say where he was going?"

"No. And he didn't have anything on his calendar either. I checked." As soon as she said it, she slapped her hand over her mouth. Her hand, super-narrow at the wrist, had an oversize flat palm and fluffy fingers, like she was wearing some sort of glove. Her palms were covered in tiny suction cups which helped her climb walls, but for her sake, I hoped they wouldn't stick to her face.

"Pika, did you check Vaan's calendar when he left?"

She nodded, her hand still on her mouth.

"Is that part of your job? Checking Vaan's schedule?"

"Sometimes."

"Was it your job today?"

She shrugged.

"Pika, I'm going to need an actual response here. When Vaan left in a hurry, why did you check his schedule?"

I didn't get an answer. Her ears suddenly

pointed straight up, and her eyes widened. At the same time, her whole body shrank by about twenty-five percent. It was a classic Gremlon response to fear and it put me on high alert. Unfortunately, high alert for me made my lavender skin glow. If whoever—or whatever—was on its way to us was familiar with Plunians or Gremlons, it was going to suspect we were up to no good.

I wrapped Pika in a hug. She relaxed against me almost immediately and swelled up to her regular size. An attractive purple man in a Federation Council uniform rounded the corner and stopped short when he saw us.

"Sylvia!" he said. "Pika, you didn't tell me you were expecting a visitor this morning. Or was this a surprise visit?"

"Hi, Vaan." I released Pika, and she stepped away from me. She put her index finger into her mouth and nibbled on her fingertip while shifting her wide eyes back and forth between us.

Vaan Marshall was the kind of man who observed more than he let on. We entered Space Academy together with dreams of one day being in positions to make a difference. Vaan graduated and went on to do so in the conventional way, by accepting a position on the council of twenty-three.

You could say I went on to make a difference too: dropping out, avenging my father's wrongful arrest, and joining the war against space pirates, all while managing uniform inventory on a commercial cruise ship.

My way was definitely the hard way.

Vaan was my best friend, until one day he was on the opposite side of the law. No matter how hard he tried to convince me we were still fighting the same opponents, I couldn't completely trust him.

"I came to see you," I said. "Do you have a minute? Pika said you had to deal with some unexpected business this morning, and if you're busy, I don't want to keep you."

"Pika said that?" He glanced at Pika. I stretched out my hand and took hers as she started to shrink. She held tightly and, more importantly, remained her usual size. "It's okay. You're not in trouble."

After sneaking on a Moon Unit, Pika had followed Neptune home and squatted on his property. (I liked to think he turned a blind eye, but more likely he'd grown fond of her in a pet-sort of way). After he was arrested, she was on her own. Gremlons are ridiculously trusting. Pika had toughened up more than most, which gave her a unique skill set. When Vaan offered her a job, complete with furnished room and board, she didn't lose a lot of sleep before accepting. And in that moment, her loyalties shifted from Neptune to Vaan.

The first time I visited Pika at her job, it became clear that Vaan had had a secondary motivation for hiring her that included me. Considering his role in Neptune's lock-up, he couldn't have expected anything more than a polite maintenance of the status quo. But Vaan was smart. He had restricted visitation to Neptune to those he approved, and he made it clear that as long as Neptune's case was under review, anyone connected to his actions would not make the list.

Considering the theft of the spaceship was kinda my idea, I didn't push the issue.

I felt Pika's hand relax. Without being obvious, I studied the way they related to each other. It was clear that Pika trusted Vaan, something that would have to be necessary for her to work for him, but it was also clear he trusted her. Gremlons didn't have a malicious bone in their bodies, but their lack of focus and constant need for attention often made them poor employees. There was a reason

Gremlons usually found themselves working in the entertainment industries. They were like an entire alien species of court jesters, only pale pink instead of harlequin patterned. God help us all if they ever discovered hats with bells on them.

After assessing their body language and nonverbal cues, I shifted gears. "Vaan, do you think we can talk? Alone?"

"Sure," he said. "Pika, go get us two cups of coffee."

"Okay," she said. She released my hand and bounded out the door. "Robot!" she called out. "Rooooooobot! I neeeeeeed you!"

I tried to hide my smile but was unsuccessful. "It was great of you to hire her," I said to Vaan. "I'm sure she brings some unique challenges to the Federation Council, but she's a good kid."

"She reminds me of you," he said. "How've you been, Syl?"

How had I been? Angry, sad, frustrated, broke, and alone. "Fine. You?"

"Fine too." He shrugged and moved past me, lowering himself onto the sofa that sat alongside the far wall of his office. There was enough room on the sofa for me, too, and he gestured with his open hand to indicate that was what he had in mind. It was cozier than I wanted, but I was here for answers, and if cozying up to Vaan would get them for me, I'd do it. "In all the years that I've worked for FC, you've never come to visit me. Why today?"

I sat opposite him. My full-coverage uniform kept me from showing any lavender skin, a fact for which I was thankful. I unlatched my helmet, placed my hands on the bubble portion, and twisted, releasing it from the collar. I set it on the ground by my feet and ran my fingertips through my black hair. I had one shot at catching Vaan off guard, and I used the only thing I knew that would do that: the truth. (The truth as I would have known if I didn't have inside information.)

"I didn't originally come here to see you," I said. "I came here to file a news story about Neptune."

Vaan's skin lit up immediately.

"But there must have been a mistake, because the news banner that ran said he was murdered. I never said he was murdered. I only said he died. A murder means an investigation, and an investigation means he'll never get out."

"Why did you have Neptune declared dead?"

"So I could break him out of prison. You know

as well as I do that he's a hero. He doesn't belong in there."

"But your news brief didn't run so you came to see me to find out what happened."

I nodded. "It would have been a tactical error to go back into the Federation Bureau of Affairs and ask questions."

"If you wanted to see Neptune, you could have asked me. I approve the visitor list. I would have made it happen."

"He doesn't deserve to be in that prison. You know that."

"What I know is that Neptune thought he could act without impunity. He committed a crime and he's serving his time."

"He killed an evil space pirate, and he did it knowing his act of bravery would never be acknowledged by the Federation. I know he's in a minimum-security prison, but it's still a prison. You're fine punishing him indefinitely for a heroic act?"

Vaan reached out and put his hand on top of mine. The warmth of his body flowed from his hand into mine, and I felt my temperature rise. I pulled away, but he caught my fingertips and held. "Neptune isn't locked up indefinitely. Not anymore. He murdered a prisoner this morning, and there's no Get Out of Jail card for that."

"But murderers lose everything: their rights, their freedom, and their independence."

"That's right. And he should. I keep telling you Neptune isn't the man you think he is. The council is moving him. I'm sorry, Syl, but you're never going to see Neptune again."

4: LITA FORARI

FEDERATION COUNCIL CONTROLLED A STRETCH
of colonies called the M-13. There were thirteen
colonies, and nobody knew what the M stood for
(in Space Academy we'd joked that it stood for
"Mwahaha," the evil laugh that was probably heard
at Federation Council meetings). Colony 13
housed the prison where my dad had been kept
after collusion charges led to his arrest. But
between you and me, if I never hear the word
"collusion" again, I'll be happy, so you'll have to get
the full story about my dad somewhere else.

When the galaxy was sliced up into territories,
the council established Colony 13 to quarantine
convicts, outcasts, and prisoners. The threat of
Colony 13 kept most galactic residents in check. It

was a bad place with no personal privileges and even less freedom. And if Neptune were to be moved there, he might as well be dead.

"Is that why you left your office unexpectedly this morning? To look into the murder?" I asked.

Vaan didn't answer right away. He kept his hand on top of mine, but I felt his pulse quicken though our touching skin. I'd learned the fifty-seven verity tells at Space Academy. I knew what to look for when assessing if I were being told the truth, but with Vaan, it was tricky. He'd studied everything I had and had the benefit of actually graduating.

"I had a meeting. Last minute. It wasn't on my schedule, so Pika wouldn't have known about it."

It was too much information. Too much too fast. Why mention Pika? I hadn't. Vaan was hiding something. I jerked my hand away from him and balled up my fist. Touching or no touching, I was glowing brightly, and I wanted him to know it was anger, not affection, that triggered the change in my appearance. "You can't let this happen. If the Federation moves Neptune to Colony 13, he'll never get out. Inmates are there for life."

"That's the point, Syl. The Federation doesn't want murderers having free rein of the galaxy."

"The Neptune I know wouldn't do this."

"You didn't know Neptune all that long. And prison changes people. The Neptune you know—if you ever *did* know Neptune, which I doubt—doesn't exist anymore."

I stood up and glared at Vaan. He didn't move from his sofa. "Whatever happened inside that prison this morning was a frame job. Somebody wants Neptune out of commission, and I'm going to find out who."

I grabbed my helmet and stormed out of his office.

It was for the best that Pika hadn't returned with our coffee, since she wouldn't understand my leaving so soon after getting there. I passed her small desk, strode down the hallway, and burst out into the courtyard.

The sky was a vibrant shade of pink that faded into orange. Colony 1 benefitted from ongoing efforts of beautification. Clear, attack-proof synthetic domes covered the surface of the colony, and temperatures, air quality, allergens, and sound levels were maintained by the programming of a control panel that existed in a highly classified room. Not only was the colony the healthiest place you could find yourself, it was the most beautiful. Fiber-optic filaments were embedded into the dome, and at the touch of a dial, the colors could shift from pink to orange, from purple to blue. It was no wonder dignitaries from every planet came here to conduct their business, often staying behind when their business was conducted. The colony, though created in a lab, was a stunningly beautiful place to be.

I kept my eyes on the ground in front of me so as not to get distracted and followed the pathway back to the space-pod parking lot. Over my head, public transportation zipped along the rails, whizzing visitors from one spot to another in lightning time. Even the rails had been carefully designed and executed: they were fabricated out of an industrial-strength metal-and- moon-dust compound that reflected the colors of the prismatic dome overhead. The windows of the rail cars were mirrored, adding to the effect. Some of the tourists who came to Colony 1 simply stood around staring at the train cars then shopped for miniature scale replicas to assemble in their homes for fun.

The trains whirred as they passed overhead. I kept moving. So focused was I on getting to where I wanted to be with the least number of distractions that I ran smack into a woman who headed my way.

I stumbled to the side, and she fell, dropping a folio that hadn't been properly closed. Paperwork scattered around her legs. I glanced at it and identified the logo for Federation Council prison. The subject line was partially obstructed, but it appeared to be a prisoner-transfer notice. I repositioned my Moon Boot on top of the paper and tried to act normal.

"I'm sorry," I said. "I wasn't paying attention to where I was going. Let me help you." I held my hand out to help her up, but she ignored the gesture. She flipped onto her hands and knees and swatted the errant pages into a messy pile. When she turned to pick up the papers that had fallen behind her, I bent down and folded the prisoner-transfer notice in half then shoved it into my boot. I scooped up the messy pile of papers and stood up, offering them to her.

"Not your fault," she said. She pointed at her head. "I've got an ear infection. Haven't walked a straight line in a week." She stuffed her papers back into her folio and glanced over her shoulder. "Did anybody see that?"

"I don't think so. Why?"

"I'm not supposed to be out here." She tapped her ear a few times with her open palm. "I run the prison laundromat. There was a—an incident at the prison this morning and things got messy. I ran out of detergent and had to make a run to the supply room."

A siren blared, three short blasts, a pause, and then a repeat. Red lights swirled over the top of the prison, and then the building went dark.

The woman stared at the building and hugged her folio to her chest. After a long moment, she seemed to remember she'd been talking to me. She pointed to a swoop of pink dirt that marred the surface of my otherwise white uniform. "Your uniform is covered in dirt. Bring it in and I'll clean it for you."

"Not necessary." I slapped at the dirt. The discoloration fell off, and the uniform looked as pristine as when I'd dressed this morning.

"That's amazing," she said. She looked down at her own uniform, a generic style issued to Federation Council employees in support roles (Colony 1 was swarming with them). The pink dirt left a smudge across her torso. She slapped at the fabric the same way I had, but the stain remained. "The prison machines run constantly. You have no idea how filthy inmates can get." She rubbed at the spot with her thumb, only managing to grind the pink dirt deeper into the fibers.

This here was what we sometimes call a dilemma. Because when I'm not plotting ways to bust my mentor out of prison or working on a Moon Unit as the uniform lieutenant, I'm a part-time sales rep for Century 21 Uniforms. The space pod I parked in the lot belonged to them, and the one thing I hadn't worked out was how I was going to explain using Century 21 resources while on my personal time.

Problem solved.

I held out my hand. "I'm Sylvia Stryker. I work for a tech-focused uniform supplier. I'd love to talk to you about our uniforms, maybe give you a demo to test for us?"

"Lita Forari," she said. "Prison Laundress."

We shook hands. "This is a special fabric that was developed for maximum movement with minimum weight." I did a deep knee bend to illustrate the fabric's flexibility. "The garment is more durable than it looks. There's a patent-pending molecular coating applied to the fibers before they're woven on the loom that makes dirt and stains a nonissue. Watch." I scooped up a handful of chalky pink dirt, pressed it onto my sleeve, and rubbed it in.

Lita gasped. I smiled. I turned my hand over so the back of my glove was against the uniform, gently buffed the spot, and then revealed the clean fabric.

"That's amazing," she said. She spoke a bit louder than necessary, which I attributed to her ear infection. A group of people nearby turned to look at us. Lita seemed not to notice. "I'd love a uniform like that."

"I can messenger you a sample. Do you think they'd consider switching suppliers?"

"I don't know. You can get me one?"

"Sure."

Lita gave me her contact information at the prison and I promised to send her one later today. We said goodbye. Lita turned away and scurried along the path with her head down, knocking into two additional people before reaching the doors to the main building.

I headed to my space pod, where I secured all doors before reviewing the paper I'd stuffed in my boot. It was a prisoner-transfer notice, all right. Someone in Federation Council was pulling strings to make things happen fast. The official-looking paperwork initiated the transfer of an inmate from the Federation Council prison to an undisclosed facility. But for all the details that were supplied, there was one thing that wasn't: the identity of the prisoner in question.

Except—there was something off about the paperwork. I held it up, backlit by the artificial sunlight, and discovered something I otherwise might never have seen. The name on the paperwork wasn't missing, it had been removed. And with the bright light shining through the document, I was able to read what someone had tried to hide.

The prisoner being moved was Neptune, but someone had wanted to keep that a secret.

5: ANGIE ANDERSON

I'd learned all I was going to learn from the prisoner transfer notice. Like everything else that had happened in the past hour, I'd collected bits and pieces of information, and if I were going to make sense of it all, I needed time to plug it into a computer, weigh variables, simulate potential next moves. The Moon Unit computers were barely powerful enough to keep up with the uniform inventory, but I lacked other options. I headed toward my space pod and my communication device rang. I held my arm up and answered without thinking. "Stryker," I said.

"Sylvia? It's Angie. How many times do I have to tell you not to answer with your last name?

You're going to scare off customers if you keep acting like you're on some sort of mission."

Angie Anderson was the owner of Century 21 Uniforms. She was a former pop singer who'd made as much of a name for herself from her self-designed costumes as her set list. After the cliché of substance abuse on the road, she dropped out of the limelight and cleaned up her act. She partnered with a textile supplier, registered a patent on Stealthyester®, and started her own uniform company. She was a surprisingly smart businesswoman, but if she hadn't recruited me to test drive uniforms for Moon Unit Corporation, our paths might never have crossed.

Ever since coming up with Operation Neptune's Dead, I'd been dodging Angie's calls. "Angie. Hi. Were you trying to reach me? I've been out of range for most of the day."

"You can't be out of range. I passed your space pod in the Colony 1 visitor parking log."

"You're on Colony 1?"

"Yes. Meet me in the quad for a touch base."

Angie liked to pretend I worked for her because it made her look more credible when she said things like "staff meeting" and "brainstorm with my team." She handled design, outsourcing, distribution, sales, and marketing. Some might say she did everything. I didn't say that, because if I did, she might wonder why she paid me, and I'd be cut off from my never-ending supply of prototype uniforms.

I crumpled the prisoner transport paperwork, tossed it in a nearby waste receptacle, and strode to the quad. All around me, tourists snapped pictures of one another in front of scenic backdrops. I always wondered what families did with those pictures. Did anybody ever look at them again?

Angie was waiting impatiently (if her foot tapping was any indication) for me on a public park bench. Her platinum blond hair stuck out in every direction, and a long strip of fabric was wound around her head. A huge blue ball dangled from her left ear, and a yellow cube swung from the right. Her white uniform was a size too small for her middle-aged body, and her cleavage burst out above the zipper. While I approached, she stood up and posed for a group of girls who seemed to recognize her from her pop-star days.

"Angie, hi. Did I forget about a staff meeting?"

Angie sat and tapped the seat next to her. "No.

I spent the day knocking on doors of Colony 1. The factories are breathing down my neck for orders, and if I don't give them something soon, we'll lose our spot in production."

"The last time they threatened to give up our spot, you gave them a stock order. Can't we do that again?"

She rolled her eyes. "Sylvia, Sylvia, Sylvia. That's not how the laws of supply and demand work." She crossed her legs and hiked up the top of her uniform. "We create demand when there's no inventory. Companies order uniforms. We produce the uniforms. Demand feeds supply. If I have a warehouse filled with generic uniforms, then we have supply and no demand. Do you see the problem?"

"Yes, but—"

"Demand feeds supply," she continued. "Supply cancels demand. We have to make the uniform-wearing public want what we have before we give it to them."

These were not the kind of lessons I learned at Space Academy. And even though my parents owned the most profitable dry ice mine in the galaxy, the laws of supply and demand went out of whack when my dad was arrested. It didn't matter what we did; our regular customers found a new supplier for their dry-ice needs.

"I thought the company was doing well."

"Ever since the MPs went on strike, our orders are down." She jabbed my chest with a pointy pink fingernail. "Your job is to get out there and get them up. I'm counting on you. Please tell me you have good news."

"I might have a lead. Do you know who provides uniforms for the Federation Council Prison?"

She scoffed. "We don't dress convicts."

"I'm not talking about the inmates. I'm talking about the employees. I met the laundress today, and she was interested in my prototype—"

Angie cut me off. "The Federation Council is notoriously cheap when it comes to supplies. What else do you have?"

I had nothing. Truth be told, I didn't take the part-time sales responsibilities all that seriously, probably because Angie wasn't all that consistent about paying me. My spare time had gone into finding a way to save Neptune, and that meant my routine sales calls had waned. "I left my contact information with a woman at the Federation Bureau of Affairs." (Technically not a lie.)

"What about Moon Unit Corporation? Who does their uniforms?"

"I don't think I'm the best candidate for approaching Moon Unit Corp for new business."

"Nonsense. You work for them, too, right? You're more qualified than most. Make a recommendation. Better yet, write up an order. You're the one who would sign off on it, right? Write it up, submit it, and see how far it gets." Angie leaned her head back and closed her eyes. A wash of color reflected from the dome covering the colony and made her cheeks appear flushed.

"Me selling to Moon Unit Corp is a conflict of interest."

"Then get me a meeting with their buyer, and I'll handle it myself." She glanced at my uniform. "And clean off that coating of pink dirt. You represent my company. I have standards." She stood up, put her hand inside the collar of her uniform, and adjusted her boobs so her cleavage was accentuated. "Call me when you get an order." She turned around and left.

It had been a busy morning, and my brain was on overload. A simple plan to have Neptune declared dead had gotten overly complicated, and I didn't know which way to turn. Selling uniforms was the furthest thing from my mind.

My rational Plunian brain usually kept me focused and task oriented. It was what propelled me ahead at Space Academy: the ability to work on a mission without fear or emotion. That skill set had served me well until personal events destroyed my life and my emotional human side reared its ugly head. I discovered that missions weren't instructions carried out on paper. I learned there are opposing forces, scary, greedy, diabolical entities that will use whatever they can to win, regardless of the carnage. That was when I first felt fear: when I finally understood that following orders with a clear, calculating mind did not ensure success.

Things were piling up, and my emotions were getting harder to keep at bay. In the past, Neptune was the one I turned to for general brainstorming.

Scratch that. Before my first trip on a Moon Unit, I didn't even know Neptune existed. I'd gotten through my formative years into adulthood with bartering, hacking, and the occasional bribe of a corrupted official. When Neptune and I crossed paths, he didn't believe I had the skills to investigate crimes or run security ops on missions. I proved it to him over and over and over.

But this time proving something to Neptune wasn't about bragging rights or self-determination. It was about life or death. *His* life or death. And that made this mission more personal than the others. That's what scared me the most.

6: FENG SHUI

After meeting with Angie, I checked the status of Moon Unit: Mars. The inspection had been delayed, and the departure clock was now set twelve hours in the future. Passengers might appreciate the extra time on Colony 1, but I had bigger fish to fry. I flew my space pod to the nearest wormhole and arrived at Neptune's ranch house on Quaoar, a planetoid in the Kuiper Belt. Quaoar was habitable only to those willing to rough it, which made it perfect for those who wanted to keep a low profile.

Having access to Neptune's network made my life easier and being able to steam open his mail gave me insights into the man that would have normally taken centuries to uncover. Did I feel guilty for the intrusion? Heck no. Neptune still knew far more about me than I'd ever know about him. In terms of digging into his background, I was just getting warmed up.

When I first moved into Neptune's ranch, I tried to respect the way he lived. I watered the plants. I dusted the shelves. I hacked into his banking account and paid the bills. It didn't take long to recognize the futility of my actions. Neptune wasn't going to know if I cleaned up after myself, and even if he did, he probably wouldn't care. I slowly adjusted his living space so it suited me. Plus, because I'm handy, I made a few modifications that any sane person would have agreed were necessary.

I canceled the utility bills and moved some of his money to interest-bearing, off-planet accounts. I bartered at local trash dumps for the supplies needed to build a solar energy pod and installed it on Neptune's roof. I retrofitted it with an antenna that I boosted with radio and Wi-Fi signals and spliced router access from an unsuspecting neighbor three hundred miles away. I hacked into the dark web and used only privacy windows for my searches so nothing I did could be traced.

And I rearranged the furniture. Neptune didn't

know anything about flow.

I parked on his helipad and let myself in through an underground tunnel that took me past his supply bunker. I grabbed two meal bars and a jug of powdered Tang and carried them to the kitchen, where I prepared myself a meal. It was the middle of the day, and too many promises of food had been unfulfilled for me to go without eating.

So. Not. Satisfying.

The nutrients, though not tasty, served the necessary purpose of focusing my brain. My day was shot, my one goal unachieved. My plan had seemed sound at the time, but the problem wasn't with my plan. It was with the unexpected murder of a prisoner. In all the confusion, me thinking the Federation Bureau of Affairs had made a mistake and classified Neptune's "death" as a "murder," I hadn't stopped to consider one thing: someone inside the prison was dead and Neptune was taking the fall. Until this moment, I hadn't considered the identity of the victim.

I settled into Neptune's most comfortable chair and accessed the information network. First, I spoofed my location to keep anyone monitoring Neptune's digital imprint from becoming suspicious, then I searched the news database. The truth was I couldn't imagine Neptune killing anybody who wasn't a threat. He was military trained and at one time so highly regarded that he was asked to be a guest lecturer at Space Academy. His actions were sometimes mercenary, but they were always backed by motivation and a need to do good.

I'm thinking you could use a little history, so here's Sylvia and Neptune: the nutshell edition. The first time I met Neptune, I wasn't a fan. I'd hacked my way onto a Moon Unit cruise ship as the replacement uniform manager, and as the ship security officer, Neptune was quick to sniff out my scam. A dead body in the uniform closet complicated things, and for a while, Neptune and I were on opposite sides of the Operation Arrest Sylvia Stryker mission. By the time the dust settled on the murder investigation, a lot of other stuff went down, not the least of which was my awareness of an unexpected attraction to the same man who'd wanted to lock me up.

Neptune was a towering mountain of muscle. He was well over six feet tall, with broad shoulders, chiseled cheekbones and jawline, tawny skin, and a rare smile that turned my knees to jelly. More to the point, the smile made my skin glow. During a recent mission, it became clear that I glowed more around Neptune than anyone else we'd encountered and not because of the danger we faced.

I was no innocent. Vaan Marshall had been the one to teach me about love in the carbon monoxide caves on Plunia. But Neptune was something different. He infuriated me, excited me, challenged me, and scared me. We'd shared a moment on the Moon Unit 7.2, somewhere outside Saturn, between him seeing me naked and me seeing him arrested. I'd lost everything: family, planet, home. Neptune was as alone as I was. But when we were together, I felt like I found where I belonged. Whenever I thought about how he made me feel, my stomach twisted, my lavender skin lit up, and I wanted to run in the other direction.

Clearly, you see why I felt compelled to rescue him.

I typed in a command to bypass the security screen and accessed the recent news bulletins. I turned off all filters so I could see everything filed, whether it had been approved or not. It took a moment to wade through incomplete reports of missing persons and news items about increased prices at the commissary on Venus and an overdose epidemic on Mars to get to the notice I'd filed this morning. It sat, unpublished in the queue. If there were any residual doubts about whether there'd been a mistake, they were gone. My news item, declaring Neptune dead, had been held back. It was approved and entered into the system at Federation Bureau of Affairs where it had ejected from the queue.

But the system was automated. It should have gone live. By the time I sat with my cup of tea in the courtyard outside of the Federation Bureau of Affairs, it should have been scanned into the system, had its details extracted through artificial intelligence, and programmed into the news stream. In fact, the only way it could have not made it into the news stream at this point was if someone had stopped it manually.

I sat back and remembered watching the news banner, waiting for my report to stream. I remembered seeing the bulletin about a murdered prisoner and thinking the artificial intelligence that scanned news bulletins and composed the headlines had made a mistake.

It was Tulsa who showed me the conflicting report that triggered the new headline. And what had she said? Another report was filed around the same time as mine. One that held conflicting data. She tried to reject mine, but it was too late. The computer initiated a conflict report and ran with the more salacious of the two stories. That meant the conflicting report should be near mine in the database.

And there it was. Six entries below mine, a news bulletin filed by a Federation Council guard that announced the murder of a prisoner. It was that announcement that led me to think Tulsa had simply made a mistake. The bulletin didn't provide the identity of the victim, and I'd jumped to conclusions.

Rookie error. That lesson was in Tactical Training 101. You know what you know. That's it.

I searched the news database for a follow-up report that told me more, but there was nothing. It was as though the announcement existed in a vacuum. It was possible that nobody else in the galaxy cared about the identity of a murdered prisoner or the circumstances surrounding his death, and the AI program had stripped out all nonessential facts. But a prisoner was still someone, and someone had to know his identity.

I minimized the window with the news database and opened another window on the dark web. I cued up a real-time search window. Questions and answers filled the screen, conversations that trafficked in anonymous information. Text disappeared as the Q&A scrolled upward and new questions replaced them. It was close to impossible to pick up random information on a dark-web search window, since it moved so fast. This was how it functioned. You typed in a question, got an answer, and moved on, all in the space of a few seconds.

I typed in: >>*requested identity of murdered prisoner in FC jail*

The response came immediately: >>*Cosmos Corsair*

In a matter seconds, new conversations replaced my question and all evidence that the exchange of information had taken place was gone.

And I knew right then and there that what I knew wasn't what I thought I knew. Because the one thing I knew was that Neptune wouldn't go rogue and murder another prisoner unless he considered that prisoner a threat.

Cosmos Corsair was the biggest threat the galaxy had ever known. If Neptune had the chance, he'd take it. And if he was caught, no way would he be getting out alive.

7: COSMOS CORSAIR

Cosmos Corsair was the OG of space pirates. He was responsible for introducing HAx5, a synthetic drug, into the water supply of three celestial bodies, introducing a hallucinogen so strong one out of five who took it became addicted instantly. The street value was too rich for most residents, which turned the addicts into criminals. Those criminals moved up from petty theft to violent crimes, often working on behalf of Corsair in exchange for more illegal substances. The Federation Council prisons quickly became so overrun with his victims that special detention centers designed for the correction and treatment of them were constructed on Phobos and Deimos, the two moons of Mars. It made sense to house them there. The moons were named after Panic and Terror, the very emotions that manifested in the addicts who couldn't get a fix.

The drug epidemic started out quietly, until one death turned into two, and two turned into four. Soon, able-bodied men and women dropped like flies. Scientists were pulled from existing projects to determine the cause of death, and before you could say "evil overlord space pirate," the evidence pointed back at Corsair.

If Neptune killed Cosmos Corsair, he'd done the galaxy a favor. Residents of every planet in the galaxy (and probably a few in the galaxy next door) would break out the bubbly, turn up the light show, and party like a quarantine had been lifted. But with the pirate's name withheld from the news report, no celebration would take place. It was a story that would come and go and get barely any attention from the public. There was a reason Corsair's name had been withheld from the news reports. Someone didn't want it known that he was dead.

On a recent mission, I'd heard rumors from a trusted source that there was suspicion of corruption in the Federation Council. It wasn't something I'd heard before, but that wasn't surprising. Most of the residents went about their lives accepting that the council was looking out for them. So much of how the M-13 was run depended on acceptance by all residents that the status quo was being maintained. If you didn't do anything wrong, nobody bothered you. There was no reason to ask questions.

From as early as I could remember, I'd wanted to work in security. I showed enough of a natural skill set to get good grades and a fast-tracked pass to the right kind of education. More recently, when the entire species of Plunians had been destroyed, Federation Council had generously arranged temporary housing and help to rebuild our lives. And even though it sounded great, I saw the offer as a mechanism of control.

I didn't know how any Plunians moved into temporary Federation housing, but those who had were in Federation Council's debt. I wondered at the value of that to a government body. The gesture read like good press, but there was something at the core that unsettled me. That Federation Council had recruited a whole bunch of purple people to do whatever was asked.

For all the good Neptune had done, he'd made enemies in Federation Council. Maybe he killed

Cosmos Corsair, and maybe he didn't, but right now, that didn't matter. Because suspected killers didn't sit around in minimum-security prisons waiting for a verdict. They were moved to secluded prisons and were never heard from again. And that meant, for everything I didn't know, I knew one thing: I needed a new plan.

I also needed some help. And with Neptune out of commission, my options were severely limited.

TWO HOURS LATER, I SHARED NEPTUNE'S SOFA with Zeke Champion. Zeke was the son of a spaceship repairman and an expert on hacking, drone technology, and breaking encrypted code. We met at Space Academy and stayed friends after I dropped out. He was laid-back in a way people with less confidence were not, which I'd learned was a side effect of being good at everything he did. I trusted Zeke with my life, and in at least one case, he'd demonstrated that my trust wasn't misplaced.

I told Zeke everything, from the plan to have Neptune declared dead to the murder of Cosmos Corsair.

"Can we go through it again " Zeke asked. "I still have questions."

"Sure. I went to the Federal Bureau of Affairs this morning to have Neptune declared dead, but after I filed my claim, a conflicting report said Neptune murdered another prisoner. That rendered my info obsolete. The new report didn't mention the victim was a legendary space pirate."

Zeke whistled. "You are a magnet for space pirates. You know that?"

"Not this time. This one's dead. I'm pretty sure magnets only attract live things."

"Do you think it means something that Corsair's name wasn't in the report?"

"I can't see how it doesn't. It's a news bulletin. Not mentioning the name 'Cosmos Corsair' is burying the lede."

"No joke. I can come up with twenty people who would want him dead without giving it any thought."

"Me too. But the bigger question is, what was Corsair doing in a minimum-security prison? He's a bad dude. He's been behind more murders than there are moons in the solar system."

"How many moons?"

"Sixty-three."

"How many murders?"

"Sixty-seven. Known."

"That's a bad dude, all right."

"He's a prime candidate for maximum, never-gonna-see-daylight lockup. Not only that, but he's good PR for Federation Council. Show him in a penal colony. Show him shackled to a bunch of other bad dudes. Show him paying for his crimes. But don't hide him in a country-club prison two hundred feet from the galaxy's governing body."

Zeke sat forward. "I think you're onto something." He spun the computer toward him, and his fingers flew over the keys. About thirty seconds later, he looked up. "The prison has a record of Corsair having dinner in the commissary last night. That means the timeline of his murder is probably right."

"Which means whoever killed him was in the prison this morning," I said.

"Assuming Neptune wasn't the killer, who else do we have?"

"Every prisoner inside."

"But you said this isn't a prison filled with murderers." Zeke's fingers flew over the keys again. "The list of crimes these guys are locked up for are laughable. Embezzlement. Counterfeiting.

Vandalism. Three different inmates are serving time for cheating on their taxes. Neptune's crime was grand theft spaceship. These aren't the type to shiv a guy for taking the last banana."

I stared at Zeke, confused. "Are bananas popular in jail?"

He shrugged. "My dad found a stash of paperbacks stuffed in the air ducts on Jupiter. I'm reading my way through a series about gangs on Earth. My point is the people locked up in Federation Council prison aren't killers."

"Neptune is."

"Neptune's former military. He has that single star on the back of his dog tags as recognition for conducting a mission that crippled a space pirate's army. That's the stuff of heroes, not murderers."

Zeke was referring to a secret designation in covert space military black ops. The highest accolade was a single star embossed on the back of a military man's dog tags. I'd seen the star myself. I'd even worn those dog tags on a chain during the last Moon Unit mission, until Neptune was arrested. (I didn't tell a soul that before the MPs took Neptune away, I slipped them into his uniform pocket. I didn't know if he knew. I didn't know if Federation Council confiscated them. For all I knew, they'd fallen out during transport—or worse, were collecting dust with the rest of his personal effects.)

"Right. So why is he in jail at all?" I asked.

"Seems to me you already know the answer to your own question."

I did. "Somebody wants Neptune to serve time. They want him out of commission for good. And this—setting him up as a murderer while inside—is precisely what it would take to make sure he never gets out. Somebody murdered a very unlikeable prisoner and set up Neptune to take the fall."

"It could have been anybody."

"It was either one of two things: somebody had a beef with Corsair, or somebody wanted to get Neptune out of the picture," I said.

"There's one other possibility. Neptune killed him."

I'd already dismissed that possibility. "I don't think so. Neptune operates from a position of defense. He wouldn't kill someone unless they were a threat that needed to be taken out, and if that were the case, it would be public. Something about this stinks. There must be someone else."

And I remembered one: the woman who ran the prison laundromat. Lita had the prisoner transport paperwork with Neptune's name removed. And her behavior seemed—what was it—fidgety? Nervous? Guilty? Like she was hiding something.

I pulled her card out of my pocket and checked the address. "Wait here," I said. "Don't touch anything. Don't move anything. Don't take anything." I took two steps away from the sofa and turned back to scan the room. "On second thought, can you move those two rocking chairs toward the eastern wall?"

While Zeke was doing battle with Neptune's seating options, I sent a sample request to the uniform manufacturer and arranged for it to be sent to Lita's attention at the prison.

Lita was close enough to my size that the uniform I sent came from my prototype stash. What Century 21 Uniforms didn't know (and what wouldn't hurt them) was that I'd made a few customizations of my own. In the lining of my uniforms was a data chip that recorded twenty-four hours of activity and then transmitted it to an off-planet server. (I was becoming an expert in off-planet resources). In the event of my death, disappearance, or detention, a passcode would self-generate and be sent to the only two people I thought would care: Neptune and my dad.

Not knowing which corner of the galaxy my dad was currently in lowered the chances he'd get the message, but after learning the truth about him, I knew I had to try.

I finished the uniform requisition and found Zeke back on Neptune's sofa, playing on a game console. The rocking chairs were in the middle of the room, having been abandoned halfway through Zeke's task. "Neptune's got some next-level military games," he said. "I've never seen ones like this."

I grabbed the game controller from Zeke and held it out of reach. "Those aren't games. They're military ops. Neptune ran those missions. For all I know, he designed them. They simulate outcomes and send them to teams before they're deployed so the parties involved know what to expect."

I practically saw the dollar signs in Zeke's eyes. "Do you know how much these are worth?"

"You are not profiting from Neptune's circumstances."

"You're the one who sold off his furniture."

I waved my hand back and forth to dismiss

Zeke's weak argument. "That was to raise capital to rescue him. That's totally different."

Zeke pushed the keyboard away from him and leaned back. "You used to be fun."

"I still am. But this"—I waved my hands around—"is not fun. You've met Neptune. Would you call him fun?"

"I'd call him big and scary. You're the one who likes him."

I barely heard Zeke. An idea crept into my mind and took hold. I sat next to Zeke and pulled the keyboard closer. I opened the root directory of the program Zeke had activated and typed in a series of variables: Federation Council Prison, Cosmos Corsair, Neptune, Murder, Extraction, Corruption, Success Rate.

Zeke leaned forward and grabbed a separate game controller. "Great! What are we playing? Let's be CIA operatives on Earth. That always sounds like fun."

I slapped the controller out of Zeke's hand. "I'm not playing a game." I hit Enter and let the computer run simulations.

Words flashed on the screen quickly, like half-written sentences that were testing out options that came after the verb. I couldn't keep up with what the system said, only that it was attempting to find a solution, an acceptable scenario in which each of my words were used to their best effect. After about a minute of this, the simulator froze. And then: *System Overload. Connection between data points not found.*

I pushed the keyboard to Zeke. "Fix it," I said.

Zeke, sensing my distress, slid the keyboard closer. He tapped the space bar with his index finger. The same words appeared until there was a full block of them:

System Overload. Connection between data points not found.

System Overload. Connection between data points not found.

System Overload. Connection between data points not found.

System Overload. Connection between data points not found.

System Overload. Connection between data points not found.

System Overload. Connection between data points not found.

He pushed the keyboard away from him. "The computer can't calculate a success rate because it can't find the connection."

"I know how this kind of simulator works. It takes a string of variables and works out scenarios, like giving it numbers to add to equal a predetermined sum."

"That's your problem. You gave it a string of variables but no predetermined sum. It can't compute because it doesn't know what you want it to solve."

"How to get Neptune out of jail," I said.

Zeke pointed at the keyboard. "Tell it what you want."

I slid the keyboard closer and opened a new simulation window. This time I typed in: Federation Council Prison Corruption, Cosmos Corsair Murder, Neptune Extraction, Success Rate. It was the same string of words, but by changing both the order and the commas, I was reframing the variables. I hit enter and waited for a result.

Neptune wanted for Cosmos Corsair Murder.

Federation Council Prison Corruption.

The Success Rate of Neptune Extraction from Federation Council Prison = 0.

I reran the simulator. The results came up the same.

Zeke put his hand on my arm. "You're not

going to get a different result from a computer," he said gently. "It uses logic and facts. Simulators are intended to remove emotion."

"What's your point?" I snapped.

"You don't need logic and facts to rescue Neptune. You need emotion. It's the only thing you've got that the people behind this won't see coming."

ZEKE GOT ME BACK TO THE DOCKED MOON Unit in record time. Catching a ride with him solved my immediate parking problem and gave me an opportunity to convince him to talk to his dad about using Century 21 for their uniform needs. (I wasn't hopeful.) He dropped me on the space station and took off.

After boarding the Moon Unit, logging in my credentials and verifying my identity through a series of scans, I signed into the staff communication portal. An urgent message directed me to the meeting room. What now? Uniform emergency? It couldn't be. I was on a break like every other staff member on the ship, and we'd been relieved of our duties until the ship passed inspection and departed. That my coworkers were enjoying their break while I was working on Neptune's behalf couldn't be helped, but I didn't need unexpected drama.

There was no pretending I hadn't received their summons. As soon as I logged in, my presence was sent via digital imprint to every communication portal on the ship. I logged out and went to the meeting room. The doors swished open. Inside, seated around the oblong table, sat the first lieutenants of the Moon Unit, all of whom had arrived without me.

I should say the first lieutenants of Moon Unit plus one. Because the person at the head of the table was most definitely not a member of the Moon Unit staff. The person at the head of the table had no business being in our meeting, on our ship, or out of jail.

The person at the head of the table was Neptune himself.

8: CAPTAIN MAJOR TOM

OF ALL THE LOWDOWN DIRTY TRICKS, pretending to have murdered a space pirate and then breaking himself out of jail and hijacking a Moon Unit ranked at the top. Especially because of the lengths I'd gone to pull off my own rescue mission.

"You're dead," I said.

"Sit down, Stryker."

"Hold on, I got that wrong. You were supposed to be dead, but it turned out you're a murderer instead."

"Sit down, Stryker."

I looked around the room at the faces of my fellow staff members. "Why are you all so calm? This man is an escaped convict. He's accused of murder. He's wanted in thirteen colonies and on at least five planets." (Earth had their own problems and didn't bother with intergalactic ones.) The committee members seated around the table remained quiet.

The electricity between Neptune and me crackled like magnetic wires crossed under a superconductor. For four months I'd been trying to figure out how to save him, and it turns out he didn't need saving at all.

He was right here.

Right here.

RIGHT. HERE.

I wanted to pinch him, punch him, kick him, kiss him.

Neptune stood. His hulking frame, broad shoulders, bald head, and drawn eyebrows painted an imposing figure. "Sit down, Stryker."

I crossed my arms. He didn't scare me! Except he did, a little. No need to be foolish. I pulled out the closest chair and sat down. Neptune glared at me for a moment and then lowered himself back into his seat.

The first person to speak (besides Neptune and me) was Captain Major Tom. "Now that we're all here, let's get started."

Captain Major Tom was the lead officer of Moon Unit: Mars. A former naval captain, he got the job after military experience became a required factor in captain qualification. Like most captains, he was physically fit, human, and by-the-book. He viewed the job of captaining a cruise ship the same way he viewed military operations. He gave orders and expected us all to follow them. I naturally assumed he didn't like me much, which left room for a certain amount of insubordination.

"'We're all here,'" I repeated. "We, as in him?" I pointed at Neptune.

"We as in you."

"Me?"

"Yes, Lt. Stryker, you," Captain Major Tom said. "Your renegade adventure this morning almost ruined months of Neptune's undercover work."

Undercover work? "No. No, no, no, no, no. I was there when Neptune was arrested. I saw the MPs take him away." I turned to face him. "I filed appeals at the Federation Council, and they rejected them. I had a plan—"

"Lt. Stryker, perhaps you would benefit from a debrief?" the captain asked.

"But my mission wasn't accomplished. There's

no brief to de—I mean, there's no need for a debrief. I said I had a plan, but it didn't work. Because this guy"—I jabbed my finger in Neptune's direction— "chose this morning to implicate himself in the murder of Cosmos Corsair inside the jail."

I looked around at the faces of my colleagues around the table, and none of them seemed surprised. Next to Captain Major Tom were Norman and Odam, two of the three members of the Stardust Cowboys, an independent security team who'd been retained to work this trip. (I assumed the third was off doing the job of all three.)

In the past I dabbled in security for Neptune—more so because I had insinuated myself in his business than any formal capacity—but with him otherwise detained, Moon Unit Corporation had replaced us (him) with a team of freelancers. As something of a freelance security agent myself, I felt it my duty to keep a close eye on them, mostly to make sure they were on the up and up but a little so I could talk my way into their organization if this whole Moon Unit gig imploded.

That meant five people on this ship already knew what I'd learned. As I processed their expressions, one at a time, I realized they all were looking at me the same way. As if they knew something that I didn't, as if they were giving me time to figure something out on my own. And there was only one thing to figure out. The suspicious timing of Neptune being involved in a murder rap wasn't all that suspicious at all. There was no such thing as a coincidence in science. And if it wasn't a coincidence that his murder conviction came at the same time as my death-notice filing, then that meant one action triggered the other.

Oh crap.

I addressed Neptune. "My plan to have you declared dead created unexpected problems," I said.

"Yes."

"You committed murder as an act of diversion?"

"No."

"Then what?"

Captain Major Tom spoke up. "When you filed that report, it triggered an alarm at the Galaxy News Service."

"How do you know that?"

He pointed to the Stardust Cowboy on the left. "Norman intercepted it." Norman flashed a quick smile that was less friendly than annoyed. The captain continued. "Thanks to Neptune's role in the capture and murder of other space pirates, there's a bounty on his head. If news went out that Neptune was dead, there would have been fallout of unmanageable proportions."

"I don't get it. If there was a bounty on his head, then people wanted him dead. Me getting the Federation Bureau of Affairs to declare him so would have shifted people's attention onto something new. Once he was off the books, so to speak, it would have been easier to get him out. Now he's tied up in a murder rap."

"Where did you come up with that plan?" Neptune asked. Aside from "Sit down, Stryker," it was the first thing he'd said since I entered the room. It was nice to know we were still on speaking terms.

"I found an interview in the Galaxy News Service archives. A former warden said if you wanted to break someone out of a Federation Council prison, you should forget about it."

"I know that interview," Neptune said. "The former warden was right. It can't be done."

"It *can* be done. I was about to do it."

Captain Major Tom slapped his open hand

down on the table then pointed at me with his thumb and index finger shaped like a gun. "Is this kid for real?" he asked no one in particular.

"She's not a kid," Neptune said. "She earned her rank like everybody else here." He turned back to me. "What else did you read in that interview?"

"After the guy said to forget about a bust-out, he said, and I quote, 'It's far easier to get a dead body out of prison than a live one.'" I smiled proudly. "That's where I got the idea."

I scanned the faces at the table, ending on Neptune's. We locked eyes for four ticks of the wall clock. His lips pressed together in an almost-imperceptible manner, one that I doubted anybody else at the table would notice. But I did. It was a smile.

He blinked first, twice, and then turned to face Captain Major Tom. "She needs to know what was set into motion."

"I can save you some time," I said. "I'm pretty quick. Let me guess: my notification triggered an alarm, and you needed a way to get Neptune out. You instructed him to kill Corsair." I held up both hands. "No judgment. It's not what I would have done, but I'm no fan of space pirates either. Neptune killed Corsair, got arrested for murder, and was put into solitary confinement or something. You guys swooped in and snatched him. Now he's here." I snuck a quick glance at Neptune, and then when I felt my flesh grow warm, looked away. "Bravo. It was risky, but it worked. By the time we reach Mars, the prison officials will be scrambling to figure out where you went. Congratulations, Neptune, you're back to being a free man."

Captain Major Tom spoke. "Lt. Stryker, your file indicates you were an exemplary student when it came to game theory, but you dropped out of Space Academy before completing your coursework on decoding intelligence reports. Therefore, I understand your ability to spin a scenario on the fly, but I do suggest you accept the limitations of your intel and let someone else speak."

Snickers were heard around the room. I didn't need to see who was laughing at me. I'd been laughed at before, and I was mostly immune to it. I reached down to my thigh and tapped a button on my oxygen-release tank that boosted the air quality within my helmet. A deep breath fortified me, and an exhalation calmed me, both necessary.

"Point taken. But the good news here is that

Neptune's out." Something still didn't add up. I studied Captain Major Tom. "You didn't tell him to kill Cosmos Corsair, did you? That was all a lie. Is Cosmos Corsair even dead?"

"Corsair is dead," Neptune said.

I turned to face him. "But you didn't do it."

Neptune neither confirmed nor denied it.

I turned back to the rest of the group. "Neptune didn't kill anybody" —probably— "so we have to find out who did before we reach Mars. Right? It won't be easy, but there must have been a controlled number of people with access—"

"Stryker."

"What?" I glared at Neptune. Maybe the others didn't recognize how quickly I could get up to speed, but Neptune surely did. "You didn't do it but someone else did. You want me to forget about the murder and act like nothing happened? You know that's not going to work. There's a bounty on your head. You can't live a regular life with this hanging over you. We have to bring Cosmos Corsair's killer to justice." I looked at the faces around the table. "We've only got two more days on shore leave, or whatever you people call it. Once the Moon Unit passes inspection and gets clearance to leave, we'll lose our access to a lot of potential suspects. The clock's a-ticking. What are we waiting for?"

"Neptune is a wanted man," Captain Major Tom said. "The Federation Council is within the boundaries of protocol to put him in solitary and restrict his access. We may never get another chance to free him."

"We can free him by proving he's innocent." I glanced around the room.

"We can't risk exposure," the captain said.

"Why not?" I looked from him to the two security officers. They'd been silent, but I sensed they knew something I didn't. As I scanned their faces, I came to Neptune. "What's more important than catching a killer?"

"Protecting the witness who saw the whole thing."

9: HEROES

"IF THERE'S A WITNESS, THEN WE'RE HOME free. Get him to come forward and make a statement, and the Federation Council will investigate, right? They can't hold you accountable if a credible source says you didn't do it." I looked around the room. "You all know he didn't do it, right?"

Heads nodded, not at first but slowly. I held my hands palm-side up, in a what-are-we-waiting-for? gesture.

"As long as I'm in custody, the witness is safe," Neptune said. "We can't risk anybody knowing I'm not there. The story, to everybody outside of this room, is that I've been chipped and am going into the system."

"No," I said.

Chipping was the somewhat barbaric method of inserting a chip into the base of the skull of a known felon for the purposes of tracking and monitoring their behavior. Once that chip was injected, there were only two options for them: follow the rules or find a doctor of questionable morals to conduct an off-the-books surgical procedure to remove the device. I'd had my own run-ins with the chipping method and wouldn't wish it on anybody. Not even a space pirate.

Though, come to think of it, I wondered if the space pirates were chipped. And if so, were their actions monitored? And recorded? And if I could figure out how to hack into the database that housed the information mined from the prisoner chips, could I pinpoint exactly where Cosmos Corsair had been when he was murdered and maybe get a lead?

"Stryker," Neptune prompted. "Focus." He and I locked eyes. A physical sensation crept over me, radiating from deep within my body, coursing through my legs and arms. Like that morning when I was sitting with Vaan, I was thankful for the new uniform style that kept my body covered. The intensified glow of my face reflected off the inside of my helmet, letting me know the physical manifestation of my reaction to Neptune wasn't entirely a secret.

Captain Major Tom spoke. "Neptune doesn't have a choice. He was a prisoner, and he's suspected of murdering another prisoner. Once he goes back into custody, we lose all contact with him."

"That's why we have to find the real murderer," I said with more emphasis than before. "The longer we wait, the less likely we are to find clues."

"We don't go after the murderer," one of the Stardust Cowboys said. There was an "N" embroidered on the front of his security uniform. "We walk away."

"Norman, is it?" I asked. He nodded. "I appreciate that you're acting security on this Moon Unit, but I don't think you fully understand what's at stake here. If we let the murder go, Neptune will be in prison for the rest of his life."

"Right now, the safest place for Neptune is in that prison," Norman said.

This guy was making me mad! I turned to Neptune. "You're going to try to solve this thing from the inside, aren't you?"

Neptune didn't respond. I knew him well enough to already know the answer. It didn't matter if I offered my assistance or volunteered to go in undercover. It didn't matter if I pulled every Federation Council string I had available to me. It didn't matter if I had the best ideas of anybody who'd ever been on a Moon Unit, if I had the skill set to dig up information the others never even dreamed they could access, or if I secretly knew Neptune and I shared more than matching logos on our Moon Unit jammies. Neptune wasn't going to put me in danger on his account.

Which meant I was going to have to do it on my own.

10: I WANNA BE YOUR DOC

THERE WASN'T MUCH MORE TO THE MEETING. Neptune, handcuffed and shackled (he'd kept those shackles a secret until he stood up), was escorted out of the room by two MPs (which now meant seven people knew the truth) and taken to the holding cell in the belly of the ship. Every time I tried to speak up or offer a potential course of action, I was shot down. The other attendees of our secret meeting seemed content with the job of arranging Neptune's safe transport to Mars and turning him over to the authorities—not catching a killer. Without a witness, an accomplice, or a lead, I was operating at a disadvantage.

Right before the doors swooshed open and the space military police appeared, we were instructed, in hushed tones, that everything we'd learned was confidential, and the safe return of Neptune depended on the utmost discretion regarding the top-secret intel.

It was Neptune's way to run security missions from the holding cell in the subbasement of the Moon Unit. The man was skilled at security and covert actions, but so was I. The main problem was that he appeared to have the Moon Unit staff at his disposal and the captain in his pocket. My pockets were empty.

But I did know one person on board the ship who wouldn't automatically fall in line with Neptune's plan. Doc Edison, the ship's medical officer.

Doc was the crankiest man aboard the Moon Unit. He'd been with the company for decades, and I secretly wondered if he'd had them put a clause in his contract that said he couldn't be terminated. His unwilling participation in the missions that took place during the last few Moon Unit trips hadn't seemed to affect his employment in the least.

My take on Doc was that he was a doctor first, a man second, and anything else didn't much matter to him. If space pirates wanted to bump each other off, then that was fine by him. And if some other people wanted to bump off space pirates, he'd be okay with that too. His sense of good versus bad was along the lines of most humans, and his moral code aligned with the Hippocratic Oath he took when he graduated from medical school. It was this last piece of information that made me think I could trust him.

Well, that and something I uncovered while running routine background checks on the crew. Since the last Moon Unit, Doc Edison had made some bad investments. I suppose it had to do with the accident of showing up for work on the Moon Unit that Neptune and I hijacked, being completely unaware of what was about to happen, and getting zero compensation for his efforts.

Doc Edison was as human as the next person (who wasn't an alien). He might have left Earth to work for Moon Unit Corporation back when jobs in outer space were a novelty, but he believed if he socked away money at a steady rate, one day he'd retire and live comfortably. At least, he believed it until the Earth economy crashed and he was left with a whole lot less nut than he'd hoped.

Doc and Neptune were never going to be friends. Not being military trained, Doc questioned

Neptune's authority. Doc made decisions out of health safety, not risk assessment. He was the most frequent critic of Neptune's advice, and his empathy had worked in my favor more than once. He was my best shot at an ally. It wouldn't do to blurt out Neptune's circumstances and plead for his help. I had to appeal to his scientific side.

I went directly to Medi-Bay, formulating a plan as I went. I found Doc entering notes into his computer. "Hey, Doc," I said, keeping my voice light.

"Sylvia," he said. "Staying out of trouble, I hope."

"Trying to."

"What brings you to Medi-Bay?" he asked. He looked up from his computer and narrowed his eyes. "You're not sick, are you?"

"No. I passed the Moon Unit physical with flying colors."

He sat back. "Good to hear it." He glanced at his screen and minimized the window.

I had one shot to get Doc on my side, and on the walk to Medi-Bay, I ran various possible scenarios through my mind. It was too soon to bring up Neptune. I needed to forge a partnership first, and I'd only come up with one option, largely informed by an earlier conversation with my other boss.

"Doc, do you ever worry that the Moon Unit company might not survive? That we're all one trip away from being unemployed?"

"The thought's crossed my mind, but it doesn't keep me up at night."

I twisted my hands together. "I guess it wouldn't. You've got the whole medical background thing. You'll find work somewhere else."

"What's this about, Sylvia?"

I dropped the fidgety act. "Do you ever think about private industry?" I asked. "Business opportunities? You know, side gigs to bring in a little extra money?" I gauged his reaction. "I don't think you plan to keep working on Moon Units for the rest of your life."

Doc tried to appear uninterested, but because I was trained to read people's body language, I knew I'd hooked him. "I've been known to keep my ears open for new prospects," he said.

"Me too," I said. "I have a proposition for you."

Doc immediately looked suspicious.

"I've been thinking about the laws of supply and demand. How when people want something that isn't available, they're willing to pay more for it."

"I know how the laws of supply and demand work," Doc said, annoyed.

I continued. "I didn't like it when pirates went around the galaxy destroying dry ice mines, but they did us a favor. The value of our dry ice went up. The Federation Council used that fact as leverage against my dad—"

"What are you getting at? I'm a doctor, not a businessman."

"And I'm a Plunian, and there are a lot less of us than there used to be."

"Your point being what?"

I sat in the chair opposite him. "When Plunia was destroyed, the doctors who treated Plunians were destroyed. Who's taking care of them now? This is the question that keeps *me* up at night." (Not really, but I figured I'd score points with Doc if I pretended to place a high value on preventative medical treatment.)

"Plunians don't require much sleep."

"See? You already know more than most." I leaned forward. "You said you understand the laws of supply and demand. There's a demand for Plunian healthcare and no supply of doctors. Do you see where I'm going? It would be worth something to be a doctor who could treat a Plunian. A doctor who has a working knowledge of the Plunian physiology. I'm volunteering to let you run tests on me. Work up diagnostic panels or whatever it is you do. Take blood and tissue samples. You know, the works."

"You're offering your body in exchange for something. What are you up to?"

I threw my hands up. "You people in authority make my ideas sound so dirty. It's called bartering. I want something from you, and I'm offering something in return."

"You're a pretty girl, Sylvia, and you're smart. I don't know what you're up to, but unless you have a medical emergency, you're not going to rope me into your plan. Do you have a medical emergency?"

"No."

"Okay, then. Until you do have a medical emergency, I don't want to hear from you. Got it?"

"Got it."

"Good. If there's nothing else, then I'm going to finish entering my notes into the database before Federation Council gives us the green light to depart to Mars."

I'd been sure Doc would go for my offer if only

for the potential income. I'd handled it all wrong, and now I was right back where I'd started. No free medical workup. No ally. No hope.

I left Medi-Bay and trudged back to my quarters. The Moon Unit Corporation had been numbering each of their cruises since the company launched. I'd joined them on Moon Unit 5 but knew their history from hacking into transcripts of 1–3. Moon Unit 4 had been such a disaster the records were sealed.

Security level 7, minimum.

Somewhere around the Moon Unit 7 series, the company changed their marketing plan, shifting from high-ticket exclusivity to a lower buy-in accessible to a wider audience. Unfortunately, that was the Moon Unit Neptune (and I) stole, which resulted in A) a lot of bad press, B) rumors that the Moon Unit 7 series was cursed, and C) an executive order to remove all numbers from future Moon Units.

The company decided it would be better to add the name of the destination to the ship, which had the secondary benefit of answering the often-asked question "Why are they called 'Moon Units' when they travel to planets?" (The question usually came from twelve-year-old boys. They were surprisingly curious, annoyingly persistent, and not-yet-distracted by post-puberty interests.)

The highs and lows of recent Moon Unit missions had left the field wide open for competitors. What at first seemed like a rising-tide-floats-all-boats situation quickly led to new legislation targeted at commercial cruise lines who accepted money in exchange for travel to solid destinations.

On previous Moon Units, my room had been just that: a room. It had a foldout bed, a cabinet for my belongings, and a table with chairs for dining or playing cards. A deionization chamber for cleaning and sanitizing before each shift was standard issue for all crew members. The whole of it had been about ten feet square.

My experiences on a Moon Unit weren't exactly what the company wrote about in their recruiting materials, but this time, they seemed to appreciate my presence. I entered a small, circular room with a virtual fireplace in the center and portrait-sized windows that were preloaded with videos of various weather events. Considering my body temperature issues, I appreciated the fact that one of the settings on the Customize Your Room dial was for snowstorm.

As my personal temperature reacted to the fake cues of cold weather, I undid the clips on my helmet and set it on a small, round metal table next to my small robot cat. I'd built Cat from spare parts on Plunia, customizing him with data chips, internal storage, voice-activated recording capabilities, and a catalog of feline behavior. Two seconds after I set my helmet on the table, Cat stood up and swatted at the helmet until it fell onto the floor.

In addition to the fireplace and frames that could be programmed to display famous works of art, I had a refrigerator filled with frozen, sugary treats, a shelf of electrolyte-heavy volcanic water from Venus, and a bed that was so buried in gravity blankets that you'd never know if someone was inside it.

Which, naturally, made me suspicious. Especially when the covers twitched.

I crept toward the bed and put my hand on top of the lump. The covers were thrown back and Pika, fresh-faced and beaming with the full wattage of her fifty-plus-tooth smile, jumped up and threw her arms around me.

"Syl-veeeeeeee-ah!" she cried.

Pika was dressed in a baggy light gray

jumpsuit. She'd rolled the sleeves and hems up and pinned the excess fabric crudely in place. I was tempted to drag her off to the uniform ward to fit her properly, but this wasn't the time to get distracted by tailoring opportunities.

I struggled to free my arms from her skinny but powerful embrace. "Pika," I said.

She kissed me on the cheek and then hopped from one foot to the other. "Did I surprise you? Did I, did I, did I?"

"Yes," I admitted.

She clapped. "Hooray, hooray, hooray!"

Pika had a habit of repeating things three times, especially when she was happy. And when Pika could surprise someone, she was at her happiest. Her pointy ears were standing straight up.

I took her hands in mine and held them still. "Pika, what are you doing on the Moon Unit? Does Vaan know you're here?"

She continued to hop, awkwardly, until she finally stilled.

"I had a vacation. I bought a ticket." She reached into a pocket and pulled out a digital card that confirmed it. She was here as a legitimate, paying passenger.

She sat down on the bed and clapped her hands again. "Whatcha doin'?"

"Nothing. I got back from a Moon Unit meeting, and I wanted to relax for a bit."

"No, you don't."

"Yes, I do."

"No, no, no! You want to figure out who killed the space pirate."

"Don't say that. Don't talk about that. Don't— how do you know about that?"

She pouted. "I know more than everybody knows. I was there."

"Where?"

"At the prison when the pirate was killed."

I leaned forward. Pika—for all her Gremlon genes that drove her to perform, act up, and try to be the center of attention—told the truth. It was a Gremlon compulsion. As soon as she said it, I knew it was true. She *had* been there. She'd been in the prison looking for her friend.

Take that, secret committee. I didn't need the help of the Neptune Hiders to sanction my mission to find the real murderer. Because thanks to Pika, I had another lead.

11: PIKA

I SHIFTED MY ATTITUDE TOWARD PIKA FROM tolerant to accommodating. I offered her a vacuum-sealed package of puffy blue spun sugar. She tore the package open and pulled off a piece, then sucked on it long enough to turn her mouth a charming shade of aqua.

I moved a tulip-shaped white chair in front of her and sat while she made herself comfortable on my bed. "I forgot you were there this morning. You said you went in early to visit with someone in the prison. Who was that?"

"My friend." Her pink cheeks flushed further.

"Is he a friend like Neptune?"

Her eyes widened. "No! Neptune is a big mean giant. My friend is a spider."

"Is he an actual spider?" I asked with hesitation.

"Yes. He's the main spider. He's in charge of the other spiders. He comes to visit me every week."

"How many spiders are there?"

"Three."

"Where do they live?"

"Mars." She tipped her head back and held the open bag over her mouth. There was clearly nothing left inside the Mylar packaging, but you can't blame a childlike alien with a sweet tooth for trying. I walked over to the freezer and pulled out a Plunian ice pop. They were becoming increasingly hard to find, but intergalactic distribution in the network of grocery stores had left enough of them on the shelf to meet immediate demand. Again, I marveled at the personalized attention that had been given to my private quarters on this Moon Unit. It seemed they finally forgave me my past indiscretions.

I ran the Popsicle under cold water to dissolve the protective coating and handed it to Pika. Her eyes widened even more than they had, and she took on an eerie quality, like the subject of one of those artists who painted children with freakishly large eyes.

Based on how Pika delivered her intel—not that she knew that's what it was—it would take a lot of time and even more sugar to get her to tell me anything of importance. My one shot was to control the narrative, and that meant keeping her distracted enough to not think too hard.

"What time do you normally go to work every morning?" I asked.

"Eight. Sometimes seven, sometimes nine. Sometimes I go in at eight-oh-five. Sometimes I get there at seven fifty-five. One time I got there at seven fifty-nine, and it turned into eight! And one time—"

"What time did you get to work this morning?"

"Six forty-seven."

"Why so early?"

"I wanted to go to the prison to see my friend."

"The spider."

"Yep." She stuck her blue tongue out and dragged it along the surface of the popsicle. "But he wasn't there."

"I suppose it's hard to be friends with a spider."

"Not for me," she said proudly. Thanks to the Popsicle, her teeth were blue too. "He likes when I meet him. I talk to him about all kinds of things. I talk to him about my job, and I talk to him about my friends, and I talk to him about the Moon Units. He's a great listener."

I wandered around my room, only half paying attention. I didn't have a problem with her befriending anything alive. In some ways, Pika talking to a spider wasn't that different from me talking to her. Sure, she responded verbally, which an eight-legged creature could not. But the content of her side of a conversation often confused things more than they'd been or contributed enough extraneous words to bury any pertinent facts. Still, it was nice that she'd made a friend.

The thought of Pika at work brought me back to my initial thought. She'd been at the prison the morning of the murder. And she'd said she went down there to talk to her friend. I glanced up at her as she sucked the last of the Popsicle off the wooden stick. She'd now had a bag of puffy spun sugar and a Plunian Popsicle, and her string-like frame had a small protrusion at her tummy. Pale-blue artificial coloring was smeared around the outside of her mouth. There was a smudge of blue on her forehead too. I had no idea how she'd managed that.

I sat down on the foot of the bed. "Tell me about this morning. Did you talk to anybody else while you were there? Did you see anything? Did anybody see you?"

I forgot that too many questions in a row caused Gremlons to gloss over. That, plus an extreme amount of sugar in a narrow window of time, caused one unwanted reaction. Pika closed her eyes and fell backward, passing out on my bed.

That was great. The one source I had for intel was unconscious, and it was all my doing. There wasn't time to sit around waiting for her to sleep it off. I needed to know what she knew so I could get on with my plan.

Pika weighed about fifty pounds, more than I'd like to carry around on a regular basis, but not so much that I couldn't move her with effort. I turned around and draped her arms over my shoulders, leaned forward, and carried her, slung over my back, to the deionization chamber.

I stripped off her ill-fitting jumpsuit and propped her against a wall, sealed the door, and turned the dial to the Revive setting. I slapped my open palm against a giant black button and watched as a blend of naturally cold difluoroethane, trifluoroethane, and tetrafluoroethene enveloped her. Before the interior walls of the chamber fogged up, her eyes popped open. A burst of oxygen followed, balancing out the breathable air quality in the chamber. The thirty-second cycle completed with a finishing blast of neutralizing hydroxypropyl beta-cyclodextrin to trap any volatile molecules that had been released in the process. When the door latch released and Pika stepped out, her eyes were wide, and her skin was a brighter shade of pink than usual.

The benefit of the deionization chamber was such that it was a dry-cleaning method, so no towel to absorb pesky leftover water molecules was necessary. I handed Pika her baggy jumpsuit and stood back while she pulled it on one leg at a time. I waited for a negative reaction. I'd never forcibly placed someone in a deionization chamber before, and Gremlons were known to process their experiences differently from humans. I knew Pika trusted me, but this could go either way.

"You put me in your cleaning closet," she said.

I nodded. "I did. And I'm sorry. But I need you to focus. Neptune's in trouble because of what happened at the prison, and you're the only person I know who was there. You might not even know it, but you could have seen something that will help me figure out who's guilty. Can you remember back to this morning and tell me what happened?"

"Yes, but I'm not the only one."

"I know, your friend was there too. But I don't think he'll talk to me, so I need you to do it. Okay?"

"I don't mean him. I mean Vaan."

"Yes, I know he was called down to handle things after Corsair's body was found, but I'm talking about before that. Before somebody committed murder and before Neptune got arrested."

"That's what I'm trying to tell you. Vaan was there before anything happened."

"But that doesn't make sense. What was he doing in the prison if there hadn't been any trouble?"

Pika shrugged. "You'd have to ask my friend."

"Pika, I think it's great that you made friends with a spider. Most people are afraid of them. But unless he can spell out information in his web, I don't think talking to your friend is going to do me a heck of a lot of good."

"But he can!"

"He can what?"

"Give you information on his web!" The

calming effects of the shower quickly wore off, and Pika sat up. Her eyes were bright, and her ears pointed straight up.

I fought to control my rising frustration and leaned forward, placing a (somewhat) gentle hand on her narrow shoulders and forcing her to look directly at me. "Our friend, Neptune, is going to go to jail for the rest of his life if nobody helps him. And right now, the only people helping him think letting him go to jail for the rest of his life is the way to help him. I don't want him locked up. I don't want him to be chipped. I don't want to lose him." My voice caught on this last line. "Neptune took care of both of us after the Moon Unit trip where we met. He gave you a place to stay, and he trained me on self-defense, so I'd be better prepared the next time somebody threatened me."

"You feel about Neptune the way I feel about my spider."

"Stop it, Pika! I'm not talking about little bugs with lots of legs. I'm talking about real people."

She twisted her torso, and my hands dropped. She reached a paddle-sized hand out and pushed me out of the way and then stood from my bed and walked to the computer console in the corner. She made two fists but left her long index fingers sticking out and then pecked at the keys one by one, waking the system and logging in her Federation Council credentials.

I got closer. As a hacker, I had access to most information I wanted, but logging into Federation Council was impossible. There was something Pika wanted me to see, and it wasn't shiny or sparkly or sweet.

When she finished typing, she stood back and gave me a full view of the screen, and everything she'd said took on a whole new meaning. Because in the middle of the screen was a logo. And on that logo were the words SPIDER: Space Prison Information, Defense, and Emergency Rescue. Under the logo it said "spiders from mars."

In Pika's world, "spiders" weren't creepy eight-legged arachnids that spun webs and caught flies. They were Martians. Martians who came to Federation Council to advocate on behalf of the inmates behind the walls of space jail.

12: SPIDERS

"Tell me about your friend," I said to Pika.

She pouted. "His name is Ronson. He's a SPIDER." She thought carefully before pronouncing each of the words the acronym stood for, as if it had taken her great effort to memorize not only the meaning but the spelling of SPIDER itself. When she finished, she smiled proudly. "The spiders come to the prison and talk to the inmates about life on the outside. Her already pale-pink cheeks colored visibly. "Ronson brings me candy."

Anyone who brought Pika sweets was in for life. "You said he was there this morning. Was that a regular visit?"

"Yes, but I didn't get to talk to him because of what happened."

"Is there a way you can contact him? So I can talk to him?"

"No." Her cheeks flushed a deeper shade of pink.

"Are you lying to me?"

A small smile curled up at the corners of her mouth. "Yes."

"Pika—"

"I promised I wouldn't tell anybody about them. And I didn't! But you're not anybody. You're *some*body. You're my friend!" She hopped back and forth between her feet and clapped.

It was good to have friends who interpreted things loosely.

PIKA TOLD ME MORE THAN I NEEDED TO KNOW about the SPIDERs. After too much superfluous information, I left her with a two-pound bag of jellybeans, popped my head into the uniform ward to make sure there were no emergencies, and snuck back onto Colony 1. We still hadn't received clearance, and with the passengers and crew enjoying the extra leisure time, I took advantage of the opportunity to find Zeke and fill him in on what I'd learned.

Zeke's space pod was attached to a vertical structure fitted with access ports. They provided power charges to vehicles under a certain weight limit and allowed mobile living quarters to dock on the upper levels for extended periods of time. Zeke, being a short-term visitor, remained on the ground, his ship slightly lopsided from a less-than-graceful parking job.

I climbed in, and he swiveled his chair around to face me. "Everything okay?" he asked.

"No, everything is *not* okay." I gave Zeke the highlights from my day since I'd left him: the meeting, the encounter with Doc, the surprise of finding Pika in my room, and the new challenges that related to Neptune's freedom.

Zeke, ever unflappable, took it all in stride. "What's our plan?"

I sat back. The better part of a day had passed since my visit to Federation Bureau of Affairs, and with the passage of time came a new color spectrum in the protective dome over Colony 1. Subtle blue and purple shades softened the appearance of the sky, fading to dark cobalt–blue at the edges. Tiny, twinkling stars flashed at intervals. I couldn't help but wonder about the planners of the M-13 and how they'd reached the conclusion that a night view programmed on a computer was preferable to the natural sky.

"Have you ever heard of the SPIDERs?" I asked.

"That underground group that advocates for inmates? The letters stand for something. Hold on, I learned this in school. Space, something, something, something, emergency something, right?"

"I hope you failed that course. It stands for Space Prison Information, Defense, and Emergency Rescue. I think. They're Martians who advocate for prisoners."

Zeke leaned forward. "Why'd you ask about them?"

"Because according to Pika, one of them was in the prison this morning." I could tell from the look on Zeke's face that he needed more information. "This morning, I went to visit Vaan. He wasn't in his office, but Pika was. She was depressed because she wanted to visit with her friend, who she said was a spider. I didn't pay her any attention at the time, but I've since learned she meant SPIDER like the prison advocates, not spider like eight-legged crawling thing. Vaan wasn't in his office, so Pika couldn't leave. Don't you think it's suspicious that a person from the Space Prison Rescue group was at the prison when Corsair was murdered?"

"Maybe that's who Vaan was meeting."

"Or maybe that's who committed the murder." I didn't know enough about the SPIDERs to slot them in the ally or suspect column. I was naturally distrustful when it came to Martians, but that was informed by very specific Martians, and if Pika's friends could help us, I couldn't let the past cloud my judgment. "We need to find them. Pika specifically said Vaan had nothing on his calendar, and Vaan all but confirmed it. Whatever happened this morning, I bet Pika's friend either knows or was involved."

"The reason those SPIDERs are able to do the work they do is because nobody knows how to reach them. They have no known address. They have their own moral code. And they're Martians. They specialize in communications. One of them was arrested last year, and he hasn't broken his silence since. You might have the best cause in the world, but I don't think they're going to partner with you because they think you're cute."

Zeke occasionally played the voice of reason. I occasionally played a person with hearing loss. Today we played both of our roles perfectly. "Are you done? Because I'm a party of one, and this is more of a party-of-five kind of job. Martians and Plunians don't get along. Even if I get the SPIDERs, I'm going to need help. Are you in?"

"Of course, I'm in! But I have to go home first. Mom wants me to clean out the garbage disposal."

We'd spent too much time sitting around discussing things. I needed action. But even with Zeke on my side, I didn't feel confident that we knew enough to succeed with our mission. I didn't fully understand our mission yet, but I knew what we were about to do required more than a uniform sales rep and a spaceship repairman's son. Not that we didn't have mad skills, but still.

I left Zeke in the parking lot and returned to my room on the Moon Unit. By my mental calculations, there were multiple prongs on my to-do list. The end target was to have all charges against Neptune dropped, and the easiest way to do that was to prove someone else committed the crimes of which he'd been accused.

The Stardust Cowboys could handle security on the Moon Unit: Mars trip, and Moon Unit staff could handle the safe transport of Neptune while we were on our way. The entertainment purser was on the ship somewhere, but he probably wasn't aware any games were afoot. Captain Major Tom could navigate safe travel and ward off any unexpected alien circumstances that arose.

I had one job. Solve a murder.

Not so easy.

Not so peasy.

But I could do it. As long as I didn't get distracted.

There was a minimal amount of guilt attached to my motivation. According to Captain Major Tom, my report that proclaimed Neptune was dead was the trigger that set everything else into motion. But even that didn't make sense to me. It indicated that Cosmos Corsair, the murder victim, was a sacrificial lamb of diversion. And Cosmos Corsair had enough enemies in both high and low places that the one unifying thought around the galaxy was that he had to pay for his sins.

In addition to the highly addictive synthetic drug that Corsair had released into the water supply, he'd been behind multiple attacks on various planets. Rumors about his hand in a recent virus that had been unleashed on Earth persisted, though questions about how he'd managed such a thing from behind prison bars kept those rumors from being fully believed (or prosecuted). If it were true that there was corruption in Federation Council, then it was possible Corsair had someone on the outside still doing his bidding. That could mean a lot of things.

To me, it meant Cosmos Corsair did not have restricted visitation rights. The first thing I intended to find out was who came and went from his cell.

And for that information, I was going to need access to the ship's master computer that sat outside the holding cell in the subbasement.

The ship was mostly empty. Captain Major Tom and the Stardust Cowboys were on board for our meeting. Doc Edison was there in case of medical emergencies. A few passengers who didn't want to deboard were off playing shuffleboard or drinking in The Space Bar.

My choices were twofold: go undercover and avoid attention or dress like I was about to enjoy my night off.

Just in case, I did both.

I changed into a sleek black catsuit with reflective sequins and a hood and pulled a long, sheer, orange-and-pink chiffon cape over it. The cape tied at the neck and flowed down to the floor. If anybody saw me, they'd think I was planning on attending one of the glamorous nighttime events on the social calendar.

I slipped out of my gravity boots and stepped into soft leather flats. The shoes weighed very little, but the rubber tread on the soles gave me traction and dexterity not always easy in clunky regulation footwear.

I left Pika in my room with a sugar hangover and headed down the curved hallway to the passenger elevators. I rode up three floors, got off, changed to the crew elevator, and used my override key to get down to the subbasement. In grand contrast to the bright, open spaces of the public areas, the basement was barely lit and dark matte gray.

All attempts to design an attractive cruise ship ended at the subbasement. The walls were slick metal. The floors were concrete painted in tacky, magnetic paint that provided traction when the gravity assist was off. The ceiling was exposed pipe and duct work, and the air quality was a cheap mix of gasses that most of the crew could tolerate for short amounts of time. I knew going in that this wasn't the time to dally. Passing out would put a serious crimp in my immediate agenda.

I tiptoed through the hallway. The gravity assist on the lower level had been dialed back while the ship was docked. The treads on my shoes gripped the ground and made *squippy* sounds with each step. I slowed down and moved my feet more slowly, prolonging the sound. I slipped my shoes off and floated up off the floor. That was no good! I slipped my shoes back on, pushed off the ceiling to get back down and kept my hand on the metal bar attached to the wall.

The subbasement was quiet. With a prisoner of Neptune's status on board the Moon Unit, security measures would have been taken. Aside from the fact that I'd once been thrown in this particular clink, I knew about the master computer down here because, when Neptune was the head of Moon Unit Security, this was his workstation.

One of the Stardust Cowboys should be keeping an eye on things. Even with most of the ship, crew included, enjoying all that Colony 1 had to offer, one of them would have remained behind as a precautionary measure. It didn't bode well that their station was empty.

I soon reached the final quadrant. To my right,

about twenty feet ahead of me, was the holding cell. Beyond that was the master computer, covering most of the surface of a giant desk console. I slipped off my cape, knotted it to the rail, and tiptoed forward. *Squip. Squip. Squip.*

When I reached the cell, I stopped. Was Neptune in there? Was he asleep? Or had he broken out or negotiated some measure of freedom? I had to get past him to get to the computer. The only way to contact Zeke was from that console.

This was it. Don't get distracted. Don't even pause to look inside the cell. This was like flying a spaceship past an accident on the side of a virtual highway. Rubbernecking only caused a slowdown, and I had no time to spare.

I slipped on a pair of polarized glasses that blocked out all distracting light sources and powered forward. *Squip. Squip. Squip.* I needed the shoes for agility, but darn if that sound didn't reverberate off every single non-sound-absorbing barrier down here. I turned the gravity assist on, and as I was about to pass the cell, heard a sound. I looked inside and ran directly into a taciturn wall of muscle.

Busted.

13: FIVE YEARS

"Stryker."

Before the wall of muscle uttered my name, I knew to whom it belonged. That didn't make the sound of Neptune's voice any less unwelcome. I put my hands on his chest and pushed away from him. "Get off me!" I hissed. And then, realizing he wasn't actually on me, combined with the fact that he wasn't in his cell, scanned him from head to toe. Neptune was a good foot taller than I was, so the scan took some effort.

"You're supposed to be locked up," I said.

"You're supposed to be managing the uniform ward."

"I'm on a break." I grabbed his arm and pulled him to the far side of the console. "We don't have a lot of time. What happened in that prison? I know you didn't kill a space pirate. You had zero reason to do him in. What happened?"

Neptune, in typical fashion, ignored my questions. "Use your badge to scan us into the evacuation chamber."

"Whoa," I said, hands up. "You want to escape? There are so many potential problems with that idea that I think you may have gotten knocked on the head and lost your mind. Except someone would have to be really tall to knock you on the head."

"Stryker."

"What?"

"Focus."

"I am focused. I have a plan."

"You don't even know who you're dealing with."

"I know enough."

See, this was the problem with my relationship with Neptune. From the first time we met, it had been contentious. Him discovering me in the uniform ward impersonating the uniform lieutenant. Me claiming I belonged there. Him escorting me to the holding cell. Me getting out, going against him, confronting a massive threat to everybody to the ship, and him stepping in to clean up my mess.

From there, we shifted into the mentor/mentee thing. I wasn't so naïve to think Neptune couldn't teach me what I hadn't learned at Space Academy, and his lack of adherence to the rules of the galaxy appealed to me in a renegade, anti-authority way. But the bricks of our foundation seemed immovable: he thought I didn't know what I was doing, and I thought I had to prove to him that I did.

"Actually, I don't know anything," I said. "Bring me up to speed."

This was a strategy. I knew exactly how things would play out if Neptune and I operated the way we always did, and it seemed a waste of valuable time to do the whole you-can't-do that/oh-yeah?-watch-me routine. I hoped shifting in a new, unexpected direction would confuse him enough to get the intel I needed in order to succeed.

Let's not lose sight of the fact that "to succeed" meant "proving Neptune wasn't a murderer, catching the actual murderer, and bringing that person to justice," which was far more noble than "I told you I knew what I was doing."

Neptune scowled. "I won't involve you in this."

"Why not? I'm your best chance at getting out. Not because I can hack into the database and change the arrest report, which I could do if I wanted to, but because everybody else is focused on damage control. They want to keep you locked up and safely transferred to your next prison cell so the bounty on your head can't be claimed. That's a life without freedom. You'd go crazy if you had to live that way."

"What do you suggest?"

"I'm going to find who murdered Cosmos Corsair. Once I take indisputable facts to Federation Council, they won't be able to hold you anymore. Add in that you should never have been locked up in the first place, and you'll be back to your lair on the Kuiper Belt before you know it."

Neptune's expression softened. He stretched his hand out toward me, as if he intended to touch my face. He stopped with his fingers a few inches from my cheek. "Why are you doing this? Guilt?"

"A little. We stole a Moon Unit together. You were looking at a five-year sentence, and I walked. Even if the FC had a solid case against us, you took the fall. That wasn't right. You shouldn't pay the price for my actions."

"Is that why you think I went so easily? Because the FC had a case against me?"

"You didn't fight them. You turned around and let them cuff you, and then you were gone." Unexpected tears welled up in my eyes. "You left me alone," I said. One big fat tear spilled over and made a track down my face.

Watching Neptune be taken into custody after what we'd been through had been one of the hardest things I'd ever experienced. Our trip to Saturn had been more than a renegade mission that involved saving the Gremlons. It was where our connection had gone from feisty banter to an acknowledgment that we both felt something unexpected around each other. And instead of having the chance to figure out what it was, Neptune went directly to jail. We did not pass Go. We did not collect two hundred dollars.

Neptune put his hand on my cheek and used his thumb to wipe away the tear. "You had your freedom," he said gently. "You had opportunities available to you that hadn't been before that moment. Vaan was prepared to give you accelerated access to the Space Academy program coursework and administer placement tests to give you an equivalency diploma. You have a whole new life ahead of you. Don't waste it on me."

That was more than Neptune had said to me since we'd met. I knew what he was doing. He was minimizing the mission connected to him to give me an out.

"Vaan Marshall is a member of the same group of leaders who sent my dad to prison for a crime he didn't commit. They let my mother deal with hurt and shame and being ostracized, and she almost lost the ice mines because so many clients pulled their business. The Federation Council didn't care about us, not me, not her, not my dad. Don't pretend I'm missing out on opportunities by turning my back on them. They turned their back on me first, and it doesn't matter what they offer me now. I have no interest in being one of them."

My skin was hot and glowing. Most of me was hidden under the black catsuit, but my face was exposed, and there was no getting around that.

Neptune put his massive hands on either side of my face. His skin, rough with calluses, felt cool against my cheeks. I stared up at him. The current of attraction ballooned to fill the subbasement. My heart thumped in my chest. I was happy to have worn the grippy squippy shoes because I felt lightheaded and dizzy, and the shoes kept me grounded.

"If only you could see yourself," Neptune said.

"You know how I get when I get excited—I mean agitated. I can't control it."

"That's not what I mean. You're vibrating."

"I'm not vibrating. I'm barely moving."

"You're beautiful." He stared deep into my eyes, and I felt hypnotized by those stupid emotions that complicated everything. "I love you, Stryker."

I put my hands on his thick wrists. His skin was cold, too cold, so cold it was alarming. I tried to touch his forehead, but I couldn't reach it.

He moved his hands from my face to my wrists and held them away from him. "This wasn't one of the symptoms," he said. And then he did the one thing I never could have predicted, the one thing that I'd never seen him do.

He passed out, collapsing onto the floor outside the holding cell in a dead-weight drop so sudden I felt the ship lurch under my feet. Neptune was unconscious.

14: IT AIN'T EASY

HAVE YOU EVER TRIED TO MOVE A TWO-hundred-and-sixty-five-pound mountain of unconscious man dressed in another fifty pounds of security gear across a floor that's been painted in magnetic paint? I've pulled off some difficult things in my days, but this was at the top of the list.

In terms of security work, there were defensive and strategic rules that we'd been taught to follow. Things about learning from experience, trusting the friend of your enemy, and working with what you had. It took a moment of futility before stopping to regroup and realizing the solution to my problem lay not in exerting my energy pushing Neptune across the floor but in removing Neptune's clothes and turning off the gravity assist.

Yeah, I was proud of that myself.

Once I stripped him down to his military-issue skivvies, I let nature take its course, and I moved to the computer. I buckled myself onto the seat, which was nailed to the floor, and opened a direct channel to Medi-Bay.

"Doc here."

"Doc, it's Sylvia. Lt. Stryker, I mean."

"I already told you I'm not interested in your proposition."

"This isn't about earlier. You said I should only contact you if I have a medical emergency."

"And?"

"I have a medical emergency."

"What level?"

"Confidential. And possibly toxic. Bring your bag and come to the holding cell in the subbasement. Wear gravity boots. Over."

I cut the communication channel and reached under the desk for the secret button that switched the system from the Moon Unit operating system to the dark web. The screen went black, and a series of white squares appeared in the center. Having anticipated this problem when I agreed to continue working for the Moon Unit Corporation,

I'd already set up a system override code, which I used now. The system accepted my credentials, and I was in.

If every elevator on the ship was working at peak efficiency, Doc would arrive in the basement in less than two minutes. I opened a chat window direct to Zeke.

You avail?

>>>TOTALLY BORED. WHAT'S UP?

Need to contact SPIDERs.

>>>DOES THIS HAVE TO DO WITH NEPTUNE?

Yes.

>>>BEEN WAITING FOR YOUR CALL. GIVE ME 5

Cutting off commun—

Unexpected bright light flooded into the subbasement, temporarily blinding me. As I blinked rapidly, Doc's voice cut through the silence. "Sylvia? Where's the patient?"

I switched the monitor off. A dark, blurry figure who walked with a clunky gait approached. I blinked several more times. Doc, in heavy gravity boots he appeared unused to wearing, came closer. "That was quick," I said.

"No passengers, no distractions. I got here as fast as I could in these confounded boots." He shook his right leg. "Where's the patient?"

I pointed up. Doc's stare followed my finger to the ceiling, where Neptune floated in his underwear. I hadn't spent a lot of time thinking about how to explain that.

"I'm not going to ask," Doc said.

We stood there for another moment. I couldn't check if Zeke had something to report, not as long as Doc stood there. What I needed was to drop down to the floor and power off the computer, severing ties with the dark web and erasing the temporary history. I suspected dropping onto all fours would do as much to alert Doc to suspicious behavior as Neptune floating above us did. I flipped the screen down so it was no longer visible.

"Get him down," Doc said. He glanced up at Neptune a second time.

"Down?"

"I can't give him a physical while he's up there."

"Oh. Sure." I unbuckled myself from the chair and turned on the gravity assist. It was hardwired with a security mechanism that regulated changes in gravitational pull to avoid people and things flying about and crashing to the floor.

Neptune floated to the floor.

When he landed, Doc raised one eyebrow.

"Are you going to write him up for not being in his uniform?" I asked.

"Wouldn't that be your job?"

"I won't tell if you don't."

Neptune's discarded uniform floated to the ground. I kicked it under the desk and backed away to give Doc space to work. He pulled a scanner out of his black bag and wanded Neptune's body. He checked Neptune's pupils for dilation, pressed in on either side of Neptune's jaw until his mouth popped open, and checked Neptune's tongue and throat.

"What happened to him?" Doc asked.

"He, um, we were, um—"

Doc stood up. "Sylvia, Neptune has been all over the news lately. I don't know if he's innocent or guilty, and I don't care. I'm a doctor, and right now, he's my patient. Any information you withhold from me could mean the difference between life or death."

"He could die?"

"He could live, too, if I can figure out what happened to him."

I shifted my stare from Doc to Neptune. It was one thing to lose Neptune to the prison. That day, when the MPs carted him away, I vowed to get him out. And in the four months between that moment and seeing him at the Moon Unit meeting, even as I wondered if I'd ever see him again, I knew he was out there. All the planning, the hacking, the lies, and the sacrifices were worth it because I knew whatever was going on behind the prison walls, Neptune was still alive. And if Neptune was a live, there would be hope for the future.

If he died, hope would die too. I didn't know if I could live with that.

"We were talking outside his cell. He was already out. I don't know how he got out, but he did."

"He's Neptune. He can do things."

"Right. He was out of his cell, and he jumped me. I told him my plan to get him out, and we, uh, disagreed on some of the finer points, but then he said I looked funny, and then he said I was vibrating, and then he went down. Like a sack of Plunian potatoes."

"That's what shook the ship," Doc said to himself. He reached into his bag and pulled out a small square unit. He pressed it against the crook of Neptune's bare elbow and pressed a button on the back of it. A few seconds later, he pulled the unit away and inserted it into a portable spectrochromatographer. The device extracted a drop of blood out of the unit, and several lights blinked while it processed an analysis. The lights ceased, and a pulsing red light replaced them. Doc stared at it without speaking.

"What is it?" I asked. "You said he was sick. Is it malnutrition? Or the flu? Did he catch that virus everybody's worried about?"

Doc lowered the spectrochromatographer and stared at me. "You said he was okay when you got here? You two had a conversation? And he seemed fine?"

"Mostly fine. He said I was—" I flushed at the thought of telling Doc that Neptune had called me beautiful. "He collapsed." I'd once collapsed in the subbasement too, but I doubted Neptune's problem was a lack of oxygen. "What's wrong with him?"

"He's sick. The fact that he's two hundred and sixty some pounds of muscle and has the constitution of a horse will help him get better, but that doesn't mean he's out of the woods."

"Sick how? Is there an epidemic on board the Moon Unit?"

"No epidemic. According to his blood analysis, Neptune ingested a lethal amount of HAx5."

15: FREAK OUT

"Neptune doesn't take drugs," I said. "He's clean. You must be wrong. The spectrochromatographer must be wrong. Something is wrong!" My voice, laced with uncharacteristic and barely contained hysteria, bounced off the cold aluminum walls and echoed within the subbasement. If anyone were within earshot, they'd know I was coming undone.

Doc grabbed an injector from his bag and held it against my upper arm. It stung me through the fabric of my catsuit. A burst of colors exploded behind my eyes, and then a flood of calm washed over me. I rubbed my eyes. Doc held out a small vial of gummy pills.

"I need you to be calm and rational. I gave you a shot of an antianxiety medication."

"I'm half Plunian! We're naturally calm people. It's you humans who are always emotional. I didn't need a shot."

"You're half human, too, and this situation is causing your emotions to overshadow your pragmatic side." He shook the vial. "The shot will wear off in twenty-four hours, but in the meantime, if you get dizzy or feel like the lack of emotional response to a situation is putting you in danger, take one of these."

"What are they?"

"Sedative-neutralizing enzymes that manually override the drug I gave you. They trigger your thalamus, sensory cortex, amygdala, and hypothalamus if necessary to get you to react properly to a threat."

"And if I don't take them?"

"If you're in danger and the shot I gave you hasn't worn off, you may incorrectly assess the threat level and do something careless." Doc glanced at Neptune's body. "If you're correct, and Neptune didn't take HAx5 himself, then someone administered it to him without him knowing.

Neptune's a big guy, and he's not easy to trick. I'd say we're all in danger."

"Are there any side effects to taking them?"

"Enough that I strongly advise against taking them recreationally."

I took the vial and slipped it into my hidden pocket. I had no plans to take them, recreationally or not. What I needed was information, and I wasn't above bartering sedative-neutralizing enzymes to get it.

In the meantime, I needed my brain to be clear and rational. Maybe Doc's shot was the thing to help me focus. "What about Neptune? Can you treat him?"

"There's no antitoxin for HAx5. The only thing to do is monitor his vitals to make sure he shows improvement. We have to move him to Medi-Bay."

"We can't."

"That wasn't a request."

"He's a prisoner. He's being transferred to a maximum-security prison. Whoever put him on this ship knew what they were doing, but they didn't tell anybody. Less than ten people on this Moon Unit know he's here."

"He needs to be monitored," Doc said.

"If you move him to Med-Bay, not only will everybody on this ship know he's here, but the people who are after him will know he got out. He has to stay in the holding cell where he's supposed to be. Can't you treat him from here?"

"It's going to be suspicious when I keep coming down to the prison cell to check on a patient I'm not supposed to know is on board the ship."

A thought tickled inside my brain, and like an itch, it grew stronger. The clarity of the injection Doc had given me gave way to a series of tasks, a mental checklist that provided answers to every question that came my way. "We need a decoy."

"A what?"

"You need an excuse to come down here every day. A decoy patient would accomplish that."

"I'm a doctor, not a double agent. I treat patients. Real ones, not decoys. I can't waste my time treating someone who isn't sick. I have to be available to tend to the paid passengers and crew."

Doc didn't seem particularly happy, but he didn't say no. The injection had taken effect, and a calm, detached sense of rationality informed every thought that passed from my mind to my mouth. I liked Doc. I trusted Doc. And I respected Doc. Those were emotional concepts, and on a mission, there was no room for emotions. "Do what you can now and go back to Medi-Bay. I'll figure something out."

———

I WAITED WHILE DOC GAVE NEPTUNE A SERIES of shots, and then the two of us dragged his body back into the holding cell. I clamped a shackle around Neptune's ankle and, after we exited, turned the gravity assist off. Neptune floated up like a helium balloon, tethered to the wall with a black iron chain.

It was late. Anybody still on the ship would either be in their room or at dinner. I pretended to leave the subbasement with Doc but doubled back after he entered Medi-Bay. Because of inactivity, the computer had reverted to the Moon Unit network. I activated the dark web and signed back in.

With Pika sleeping off her sugar binge in my room, I didn't feel comfortable using my computer. I also knew the Moon Unit system was compromised. Too many issues with past trips had led to upgraded security measures that scanned search activity and sent daily summary reports to both internal management at Moon Unit Corporation and the Stardust Cowboys. The notion was that two heads were better than one— or, in this case, double the eyeballs on possibly illegal crew activity meant double the chances of thwarting said activity before it went awry.

But there were things I needed to know, and the only way to find them out was to dig.

Until now, I kept a mental tally of people I'd come into contact with since filing paperwork at the Federation Bureau of Affairs. One of those people had been the prison laundress. Lita had seemed so innocent, from the moment she crashed into me and scattered paperwork to the interest she'd shown in my uniform. But she'd had that prisoner transport paperwork. What possible reason was there for her to have it? Had she been the one to remove Neptune's name?

If so, why?

I logged into the remote server in which the personal data logs from my uniforms were stored. Assuming Lita wore the uniform sample I sent to her attention, the embedded chip would act as a listening device and help me get a read on what was going on inside the prison.

The first two segments of the data log were

empty. On the third segment, I found information. The file was audio, and from the narrow margin of sound recorded, I could easily pinpoint parts that included conversation.

There were several conversations with others about new uniform requests. I assumed that was the biggest part of Lita's job, cleaning the dirty ones, delivering clean ones, and keeping track of them all. It was about as interesting as my work on Moon Unit, and I felt pity at the monotony of it all.

But one conversation stood out. It was one-sided, which led me to conclude the other party wasn't in the room.

Transcript:

Lita: Yes, this is the prison laundry. Yes, I did. Earlier today.

<Pause>

Lita: What?

<Pause>

Lita: So far, so good. No, I haven't told anyone. This morning. Yes.

<Pause>

Lita: What?

<Pause>

Lita: I can't pay you. Not yet.

<Pause>

Lita: I'm sorry. Can you repeat that?

<Pause>

Lita: If you want to send a supply for the prisoners, I'll distribute the product myself.

<Pause>

Lita: I can barely hear you.

<Pause>

Lita: Okay. Over.

The transcript went silent. I reread the transcripts two more times. I was uncertain about a whole lot of things, but of one thing I was certain: Lita Forari had a secondary agenda.

16: MOONAGE DAYDREAM

Even with only half of a conversation to listen in on, there were too many red flags from the transcript for me to dismiss Lita as innocent. She referenced "earlier today," which was when the murder took place. She said she hadn't told anyone. She said she couldn't pay. And she offered to distribute the product herself.

I considered what it all meant. She hadn't told anyone. Hadn't told them what? That she'd seen Neptune's name on the prisoner transport paperwork, or worse, that she'd removed it? She couldn't pay. Was someone blackmailing her? Was she behind the hit on Cosmos Corsair—had she hired someone to commit the crime and was now backing out of her end of the deal?

She'd also said she'd take over distribution herself. Was she in communication with someone from Corsair's network—distributing HAx5 to the inmates inside the prison?

It troubled me that through all of this, I didn't know what had happened to Corsair's body. After he'd been found dead, he would have been moved from the prison to a Medi-Morgue where an autopsy would have taken place. Except, in the case of a prisoner, I didn't know how far they'd go with such things. Would how he died be a matter of public record? His name hadn't even been released to the public. I doubted his cause of death would.

I'd forgotten all about my idea to search the chipping directory to track Corsair's last moves. Even if he were dead, the chip would still transmit.

I'd never searched the chipping directory, but I knew of two people who had been chipped: Neptune's sister and my dad. I applied my password encryption software to the chipping database and waited while the information became available. Once in, I searched for the space pirate's name and found an interesting and unexpected piece of information—or rather the lack of it.

Cosmos Corsair had never been chipped.

He was the perfect candidate for chipping. The Federation Council claimed to be at war with space pirates. Neptune and my dad had both joined that war, and when I found out about it, I got drafted to fight too. If one of the worst pirates in the galaxy were in custody for life, the only reason for *not* chipping him was if someone planned, one day, to give him back his freedom.

Someone wanted Cosmos Corsair alive.

Yet someone murdered him.

I wanted to know both parties, but solving the murder seemed the easier task.

By my estimation, there were multiple suspects. For starters, there were inmates. About a hundred of them, by the count I found in the roster on the back end of the Federation Bureau of Affairs database. There were prison employees who came and went with security privileges: wardens, janitorial staff, delivery crew, laundry services, and food supply. Any one of them could have killed the evil pirate while he was incarcerated. But did any of them have a reason to frame Neptune?

And then there was Vaan. My former friend, classmate, lover, and fellow Plunian. He had multiple beefs with Neptune. Vaan was the one who had arranged for the police to take Neptune into custody when we landed on Saturn after saving an entire race of aliens. Another person might have given him a medal. Vaan had been hiding something when we'd talked in his office. I'd been too caught up in nostalgia and trickery to figure it out. But now, thanks to Doc's shot, I was cool as a space cucumber. I had to see Vaan again.

I couldn't help but think about Pika too. She was the sweetest, gentlest alien I knew, but she'd seen corruption firsthand and had weathered a few storms of violence herself. Taking a job with Federation Council put her into a whole different category, one in which she'd have to interact with the public, manage Vaan's affairs, oversee inmates, and be a professional. But what if she'd come into contact with Cosmos Corsair herself? Her fellow Gremlons were almost mass-murdered by a different space pirate, and Pika understood that threat before the others had. I knew how violence and revenge could creep up on you and make you want to take an eye for an eye.

When my dad was arrested, I'd wanted retribution. I didn't think Pika had the wherewithal to plan an elaborate murder and frame Neptune, but what if Corsair had threatened her? She had seen me fight back against attacks more than once, and Neptune had tried teaching her self-defense for that very reason. What if she fought back against an attack and accidentally went too far?

What if Neptune caught Corsair threatening Pika? He wouldn't sit by and let it happen.

What if Pika was the witness?

I was back to thinking Neptune did it. For all the right reasons.

But he wouldn't have taken HAx5. He wouldn't have broken out of his jail cell. He wouldn't tell me he was looking for Corsair's real killer. And with my new level-headed thinking, I remembered something Neptune said before collapsing. "This wasn't one of the symptoms."

Did Neptune take the HAx5 on purpose?

I ruled out suicide. Doc had said lethal dose but lethal to whom? One Neptune equaled two of anybody else. Plus Neptune trained religiously. He knew his body and its limitations. Did Neptune know he could metabolize an otherwise lethal dose of HAx5? What was he trying to prove?

Who else? Pika's friend Ronson had been at the prison the morning of the murder. So had Lita. So had Angie, my boss.

I hadn't given much thought to Angie's presence on Colony 1. But she had been there.

And when I offered up leads for uniform sales, she discouraged me from pursuing Federation Council. Angie had never dissuaded me from following a potential lead before.

And another thing: Angie had lost her lucrative and attention-seeking career in pop music to a substance abuse problem. How had I not considered that? Did her addiction have anything to do with HAx5? Was there a way for me to find out?

Any one of these suspects could have killed Cosmos Corsair. Any one of them could be the witness Neptune swore to protect. I had four solid leads plus about a hundred abstract ones. As focused as I was, the way forward was still unclear.

I powered the dark web back on and reached out to Zeke. *You there?*

>>WAITING ON YOU. FOUND INFO. READY?

I chewed my lip. I was ready, all right, but not the way Zeke thought.

Tell me in person.

>>???

Hope your mom forgives you for not cleaning out the disposal. Stand by. We're pulling an all-nighter.

17: HANG ON TO YOURSELF

Zeke's parents thought Zeke was an underachiever who had no aspirations despite graduating from Space Academy and spending his spare time on joyrides. They didn't know Zeke was secretly one of the most highly sought-after drone technicians in the galaxy, accepting payments in universal currency that he kept hidden in an unmarked bank account on Venus. (I told him about the off-planet banking I used for Neptune, but Zeke preferred to diversify.)

We arranged to meet by the escape hatch. If Zeke could fly into a nearby wormhole, there was no telling how quickly he'd arrive. If he didn't sneak away, it would take him time to convince his dad to let him take the repair pod again, but Zeke's dad was accommodating when Zeke showed interest in anything entrepreneurial. One day, when the truth came out, his dad would be very, very proud.

My immediate list of things to do grew longer. I not only had to find a trustworthy crew member to act as a decoy patient so Doc had an excuse to check on Neptune, I had to get to the escape hatch so Zeke could pick me up. That meant getting past Neptune one more time.

As I was powering down the computer console and removing all evidence that I'd been there, the security doors swished open, and one of the Stardust Security Cowboys entered. If I revealed my presence, I'd have to explain about how Neptune happened to be chained to the wall. That seemed a troublesome detail.

The door to the escape hatch was at the back of the hallway. I slowly backed away from the desk, my shoes making quiet but audible *squip squip* sounds against the floor. The black of my catsuit helped me blend into the background, but my lack of oxygen, bubble helmet, hacking tools, or overnight kit left me feeling less prepared than I would otherwise have liked to be. I backed up against the door and stopped to listen.

"Yo, man, you asleep?" the security guard said. It was Norman, the confrontational security officer from the meeting earlier. I was more curious about who it was he was talking to. The chair outside the holding cell squeaked. "Not sure what kind of point you're trying to make in your underwear, but to each his own."

Uh-oh. He was talking to Neptune.

I meant to redress Neptune before I left. The thought came to me like a bulletin streaming through my brain, not the panicked afterthought of a woman who was making it up as she went. Was that because of the shot Doc gave me? Was this a moment in which my natural fight-or-flight response would come in handy? My hand hovered over the pocket where the vial of gummy pills was.

But I wasn't ready to lose clear, rational Sylvia. All my life I'd been hindered by being half human. I used to think that made me relatable, but truthfully, if I didn't have all those pesky emotions to deal with and could go through life making clear, conscious decisions, then life would be easier.

I pushed the vial back down into the pocket and zipped it shut. Zeke would arrive soon. We hadn't worked out the details of how I would know he was there, but Zeke and I had a shorthand that allowed us to work in tandem. We'd developed it when we studied at Space Academy together. Until I saw the approaching headlights from his dad's repair pod from the observation deck, I was on my own. Of course, I couldn't see the headlights to his dad's repair pod until I was at the observation deck, and getting to the observation deck would prove its own challenge, so shorthand notwithstanding, my immediate future was still somewhat unclear.

Wearing black had proved to be a smart choice. Aside from the reflection of my purple face, I blended in with the walls of the subbasement. I slipped off my shoes and glided up to the ceiling. I pushed off with my left foot in a slow gliding diagonal pattern to the right side then pushed off the right in a slow glide to the left. When I reached the Control Center, I looked down. Not only was Norman sitting behind the desk, Neptune was sitting with him. Norman's lips were moving, but no sound came out. I hadn't heard the cell open, but that was to be expected, considering it was held shut by invisible beams of radioactive light. But how had Norman gotten Neptune unlocked? How had Norman gotten him dressed? How had

Norman moved him from inside the cell to the desk area without me hearing?

And how was it they were sitting in the same space where the lack of gravity kept me floating in the air above their heads?

Uh-oh again! Norman must have turned on the gravity assist, because I hadn't even noticed that I was slowly gliding toward the ground!

I stuck my foot out and hooked it around an exposed pipe. The lack of sound—which I'd experienced once before on a Moon Unit—worked in my favor. I bent toward my foot and slung my hand over the pipe, and then hooked my arms and legs around it and slowly inched myself forward.

Moon Units were equipped with sound-cancellation mechanisms for the purposes of overtaking a threat to passengers without giving away crew position. The mechanisms were built and installed on the recommendation of military personnel who had been consulted after the recent hostage situation on board Moon Unit 7.2. I only knew about it because I had an internet search programmed to me when any news about Moon Unit 7.2 was released. That was the ship Neptune and I had commandeered, and I kept apprised of all intel before forming my plan to break him out of jail.

But if I wasn't supposed to know about it, then nobody else was either. The Stardust Cowboys were an independent security firm. Would the Moon Unit Corporation tell them everything? Or was that restricted, top-level, first-officer need-to-know basis?

I could ask Captain Major Tom. Being former military, he'd know. I could try to trick him into thinking I knew all along, but I doubted he'd fall for anything short of an emergency. But there was one other crew member on board the ship who would know, and he owed me. The engineer, Ofra Starr.

Ofra Starr was a glamorous, black, three-hundred-pound crossdresser, who, unbeknownst to him at the time, had absconded from a recent cruise with a priceless carbonado diamond sewn into his otherwise regulation Moon Unit uniform.

Rumors around the galaxy (another saved internet search) reported that Ofra was now living the high life. Money he seemed to have fallen into possession of was spread back out into communities, making him both popular and prestigious. Moon Unit Corporation, fearing they'd lose a reliable engineer, bumped his rank to first officer and offered him a buy-in to the shareholder pie. Now Ofra was more than the engineer; he was part owner. All because of little ol' me.

And now, I had a way for him to say thanks.

Inching my way along the pipe, I reached the portion of the subbasement directly above the desk. Neptune's mouth moved, but the sound was inaudible. There was no tension between him and the security officer. That led me to believe Neptune was working with him.

My clearly functioning brain reached the conclusion that this was how Neptune had gotten out of his cell. He had partners on the ship. People he trusted. Which must have been his mistake. Because what Neptune seemed not to know that I did was that Neptune's overdose might not have been an accident. Maybe he did know what he was doing. Or maybe someone had seized an easier path to rendering him useless.

The clear lens through which I now processed details was amazing. Who could have let Neptune out of the holding cell? A security agent. Who would ever know Neptune had overdosed on HAx5? Nobody—unless Neptune died and there was an autopsy.

Highly decorated military man.

Eliminated a space pirate.

Visiting professor at Space Academy.

Advised on Moon Unit security.

There was no way there wouldn't be an autopsy.

As I inched along the pipe over Norman and Neptune's heads, something else struck me. Nobody would have known about Neptune's overdose if I hadn't come down here to see him. Plus the holding cell was about twenty feet from the escape hatch. Did they want to turn him into an addict? Or was the intent to kill him and then send his body into orbit with the space trash, never to be seen again?

I was beginning to think Neptune's trouble had followed him on board the ship.

18: STARR MAN

I MADE IT TO THE END OF THE HALLWAY AND lowered myself into the High Velocity Pressure Transport System. The HVPTS was a body-sized canister that used an under-foot pressurized charge to send crew members from one point of the ship to another. It was designed for use by security and top-level crew and wasn't common knowledge to anyone else. Anyone monitoring the ship schematics would know if the HVPTS had been used, but it was the fastest distance between two points, and that was all that mattered.

I reached Engineering. Ofra, as expected, was seated behind his console. His blue uniform shirt was bedazzled with opaque opals mined on Mars. (The gemstones had been discovered early in the

century and mining them had been a growth
industry ever since.) His left hand was splayed on
the desk, and his right held a tiny nail-polish wand.
Two of the fingernails on his left hand were
pearlescent pink, and the other two were blue. He
tapped the tip of the wand to the nail on his middle
finger, and the nail turned lime green.

"Lt. Stryker," Ofra said. He smiled broadly,
revealing a diamond chip embedded in his front tooth.
Matching diamonds pierced his eyebrows, and the
light from the transporter glistened off the facets. "I
should have known if I were to have company it would
be you. I've been expecting you. Come to collect?"

"Collect what?"

"Don't play coy. We both know I owe you. I
admit, I've fantasized about this moment. What
will you ask for? How much of my newfound
fortune will you demand?"

"I'm not here for a cut of your profits. Those
are yours. But I do have some questions about the
ship that I was hoping you could answer."

Ofra set the nail-coloring wand down. "Every
alien and human in the galaxy wants a cut of my
profits. Why don't you?"

There'd been a time when I wished I had that

kind of wealth. Back when my family struggled financially. Not for me but for my mother, who had to assume the day-to-day responsibility of the farm. People treated us differently, and I'd wanted the kind of power that money could buy so I could treat others the way they treated us.

"Money can't buy happiness."

"Maybe not, but it can buy planets."

I hadn't expected that. "You're buying a planet?"

"I'm in a bidding war for Pluto as we speak."

"I don't think Pluto is considered a planet anymore. Planetoid, maybe."

"My first act of Congress after taking possession is to reinstate planet status. I hired a team of graphic artists to design our new flag. Want to see?" He pulled a small computer tablet out from a shiny Mylar pouch on the floor and held the computer in front of him for an ocular scan. The opening bars of "The Jupiter Symphony" sounded. Ofra turned the screen to me and smiled. "Isn't it gorge?"

The image was a multilayered flag made from panels of chiffon. A wind simulation had been used to illustrate how the colors whipped against one another, turning equal parts blue, pink, and lime green.

"I've always wanted to go to Pluto, but I can't afford the ticket," I said.

"My second act of Congress will be to pass a bill that allows you free transport to and from Pluto. You will always be welcome on my planet."

"Planetoid."

He shook his head. "I should have put in a bid on Mercury. So much less controversial."

"But then you'd have that retrograde nonsense to contend with. Don't the crime rates skyrocket three times a year?"

"Invest in property, they told me! I'm a fool to have listened." Ofra raised his hands and waggled his multicolored fingernails dramatically. He caught me staring at them and held them steady to show them off. "I'm living my brand."

"You should teach a class." I was losing patience with Ofra. "What can you tell me about the silencer mechanism on the ship?"

"Whatever happened to small talk?" He raised his hand and snapped in front of my eyes. "Are you sure Sylvia is in there? You're acting like an automaton. You aren't a clone, are you?"

I thought about Doc's pills again. My

newfound sense of clarity and focus was great, but the trouble was with everybody else. If they would respond to me the way I spoke to them, I'd get what I needed and move on. Small talk was a waste of time!

"Your flag is gorge. Pluto was a wise investment. And that's a particularly nice shade of lime green on your middle finger."

He tucked the tablet back into the mylar pouch and then turned back to me and poked me in the chest. "You're still in there, I can tell." He leaned forward. "Is it drugs? Is that what has you acting funny?"

"I'm not acting funny," I said calmly. Too calmly, if you must know. Ofra's question should have made me anxious. Instead, my heart rate thumped at an even pace, even when Ofra leaned forward and sniffed me. "You may notice a trace of zinnia, which I put in my tea earlier this morning."

"You have zinnia in your room? I thought that was only for first officers. What other perks was I promised that are being given willy-nilly to the entirety of the ship?"

Ofra was a perfect candidate for the same shot Doc had given me. His hysteria rose in direct proportion to my calm. It was as if he felt someone needed to be emotional, and the sum of our two dispositions was clearly not adding up properly, so he overcompensated on his end. The problem was that Ofra wasn't communicating with me the way he usually did, and that, I guessed, had more to do with me than him. I pulled the vial out of my pocket and popped a gummy tablet into my mouth.

Within seconds, adrenaline coursed through my body, bursting out of my chest and flowing through my arms and legs. My feet felt like they were being pricked with pins, and I hopped from foot to foot to minimize the sensation. The same fear that I hadn't felt moments ago was all around me. Did the Stardust Cowboys know I was out here? Were they the ones who drugged Neptune? Was Ofra going to turn me in? Was Zeke going to be able to get me from the ship? Were the SPIDERs on the up and up? Were we going to crash on the way to Mars? Were the corrupt Federation Council members secretly behind a mass annihilation plan to cover up their shenanigans?

I grabbed Ofra's wrist. "You have to help me. I'm on a mission. No one can know."

Ofra smiled. "You're back."

A button lit up next to Ofra's console. "Bridge to Engineering. This is Captain Major Tom."

Ofra held up his index finger to me and took the call. "Yes, Captain?"

"Have you seen Lt. Stryker? I received a communication from an independent service pod that she requisitioned them for a minor spaceship repair job. We got the all-clear from Federation Council to depart for Mars, but if there's a problem they didn't catch on the inspection, I need to report it."

Ofra raised his eyebrow again. I shook my head rapidly. He smiled. "No, Captain, I haven't seen Sylvia. But it wouldn't surprise me to learn she's in the commissary. They're releasing a fresh batch of oxygen-infused ice cream at the top of the hour, and you know Sylvia . . ."

Captain Major Tom's voice chuckled. "I suppose she deserves a bowl of ice cream. I'll put the repair pod in holding until I can confirm. That's all, Commander Starr."

The speaker went silent. Ofra turned back to me. He leaned forward and propped his chin on his fist. "Now, what's this about a secret mission?"

19: THE RISE AND FALL OF SYLVIA STRYKER

My words rushed out in a whoosh. "Neptune's on the ship," I said. Ofra was surprised, though a recent shot of Botox kept his forehead from moving. "He's in a holding cell in the subbasement. The freelance security team is watching him. Someone administered a lethal overdose of HAx5, and he passed out."

"Neptune passed out? That must have been some drug." A silly smile played at the corners of Ofra's mouth. After a moment, the smile dropped, and he looked at me, all traces of indulgent curiosity gone. "Wasn't Cosmos Corsair the single supplier of HAx5? I thought Neptune murdered him."

"That's not common knowledge. Where did you hear it?"

"Sylvia, dear, I'm a shareholder of the Moon Unit Corporation in negotiations to purchase a planet. I hear things."

Apparently money bought more than planets.

"He didn't do it," I said.

"I wouldn't care if he did. Everybody I know feels that way. But if Corsair is dead, then who has access to HAx5?"

"The person framing Neptune."

"Neptune was framed?"

"I'm sure of it." The drug had loosened my lips, and I filled Ofra in on most of the details: my initial plan to have Neptune declared dead, the sudden news report of Corsair's murder, and current arrangement to move Neptune to Mars. I kept mention of the SPIDERs to myself. Ofra had his own reasons for keeping my secret, but that didn't buy him full disclosure.

"What's your plan?"

"Doc needs a reason to monitor Neptune, but nobody is supposed to know Neptune's in the holding cell. We need a decoy patient on the same level as the subbasement for Doc to treat." I gave Ofra a moment to figure out for himself what I was asking, but the gummy anxiety-producing drug made my impatience intolerable. "You. We need you to pretend to need medical treatment so Doc has an excuse to leave Medi-Bay."

"But I'm the picture of health."

"Are you sure? That piercing on your eyebrow looks infected."

"No!" Ofra's hand flew up to his forehead, and he grabbed a hand mirror that he happened to have within arm's reach. When he saw I was lying, he relaxed. "You're a worthy opponent, Lt. Stryker. I suppose it wouldn't hurt me to consult with Doc about some cosmetic surgery I was considering."

"You're beautiful the way you are."

Ofra beamed. "What about the space repair pod you requested? What do you have planned with that?"

"That's Zeke Champion. He's here to pick me up and fly me to Phobos."

"How are you planning to get onto Zeke's space pod?"

"Escape hatch."

"I'll do you one better. Get what you need from your room and meet me back here. We'll test out the new dematerializer."

Gulp.

"There's no time to panic, Lieutenant You heard the captain. We passed the inspection and were given clearance to depart. Captain Major Tom will make his rounds of the ship at half past the hour. We have a limited window of opportunity." He clapped his hands. "This is so exciting!"

I didn't go to my room. I went to Doc. Because the idea of being broken apart into bits of energy that were reassembled at some remote destination point —which was pretty much what a dematerializer/re-materializer did—was enough to send me into a tailspin. Even without the anti-anxiety shot, I would have been anxious. There are some things for which you can't medicate.

Doc was bent over a row of small, flat Petri dishes. He held up his hand as I entered Medi-Bay but didn't look up. He had on a special pair of extreme magnification glasses, and when he finished inspecting the dishes in front of him and looked at me, his eyes appeared so big he looked like an alien species. Considering Doc's time in outer space was a necessary evil and not a desire to spend time in the galaxy, I kept that observation to myself.

"Sylvia," he said. "Geez, you look awful." He held a pen light up to my eyes and checked first one then the other. "You're not the decoy patient, are you?"

"I need another shot," I said. "Zeke's circling the ship, and Ofra's going to dematerialize me, and Neptune's being watched by some freelancers who aren't in the system, and Pika told me to talk to the SPIDERs, and—"

"What are you on?" he asked.

"Nothing! The gummy pills. I chewed one. You said I could, and I'd be okay, so I did, and I'm FREAKING OUT!"

"Let me see the vial."

Doc's calm manner wasn't contagious. My hand quivered as I pulled out the vial. He opened it and shook a tablet onto the palm of his hand. He put it into an analyzer and started a sequence. The computer came back with a chemical composition. I waited for him to swear or apologize for giving me the wrong drug. He didn't. He was the picture of efficiency, which only made me more nervous in contrast.

"What happened? Did you give me the wrong

stuff? Or not enough? Can you give me something to calm me down? Because if I can calm down, then I can help you. I can help Neptune. I can help everybody. I just have to pick one! Who should I help? Maybe I should go to the uniform ward and help out there. Pika! Has anyone seen her? Uniforms! I'm supposed to be selling uniforms! Do you have any sales leads?"

Doc aimed a penlight at my eye. "Fascinating," he said. "You only took one of these?" He shook the vial.

"Yes."

"Where were you when you took it?"

"Engineering. I went to see Ofra about being your decoy patient."

Doc's expression changed. "Get on the table." He reached behind him for an oxygen canister and thrust the mouthpiece at me. "Inhale."

I pushed it away. "What's wrong?"

"The air quality in the engineering deck has a high percentage of nitrous oxide. There's less oxygen than in other parts of the ship."

Almost immediately, I understood Doc's concerns. I grabbed the mouthpiece and inhaled.

Plunia had air quality that was close to one hundred percent pure oxygen. The planet wasn't livable for most other species. The reason Plunians mined dry ice was because we thrived breathing almost pure levels of oxygen.

Dry ice was the solid form of carbon dioxide: a single carbon atom bonded to two oxygen atoms. Other planets used our dry ice in conjunction with their own air quality to produce a breathable mix of air that suited a wide variety of visitors. When I first left Plunia, I learned what happened when I didn't get the oxygen I needed, which was when I started regulating my oxygen intake through my bubble helmet.

But I'd left my helmet in my room when I changed out of my uniform. Wearing it would have given away my identity, and creeping around the subbasement, where I had no business being, required as much anonymity as possible. I'd breathed in the air on the ship, assuming that air was a chemical mix I could tolerate. And now, this.

After I felt my anxiety subside, I held the mouthpiece away from my face. "Why is there nitrous oxide in the engineering sector?"

"It's used in rocket boosters. The ship carries tanks of it in case of emergency. Ofra reported a slow leak. He requested a service stop at the next space station, but Federation Council denied it."

"The council denied Ofra's service request? They greenlighted our inspection and clearance to depart. It's because of Neptune, isn't it? They're putting the lives of everybody on the ship at risk so they can lock him up faster."

"There isn't much of a risk. Nitrous oxide is commonly called laughing gas. It's a free radical and is relatively benign. The worst thing that can happen with a slow leak is people are happier."

"Is that why Ofra is so happy?"

"There are many reasons Ofra is happy."

"But what about me? I didn't get happy. I freaked out."

"Your system was already compromised because of the shot I gave you. The gummy pill should have allowed a naturally occurring dopamine spike into your system. That pill opened a window for your anxiety, and the nitrous oxide reacted with you differently than it would have someone who was used to breathing mixed air quality. You metabolized it rapidly, and that small, naturally occurring spike of dopamine translated into a wallop of adrenaline."

"Which means what?"

"You freaked out."

Doc held out an oxygen tablet and a cup of

purified water. I glanced at it and clutched the oxygen tank to my chest. "I'd rather not take more pills," I said.

He withdrew his hand and set the tablet and water on the counter behind him. "If only more people had your common sense, we wouldn't be facing a drug epidemic."

I hadn't spent a lot of time thinking about the drug epidemic at the center of Cosmos Corsair's incarceration. "What you explained to me about how I metabolized the nitrous oxide, is that how HAx5 works?"

"Close. The pill magnifies the feeling you get when you're happy. It's like a dopamine hit times a hundred. It interacts with normal brain functioning. Users report experiencing perfection. Some call it a love drug. The galaxy is beautiful, life is satisfying, and personal interactions are deep and meaningful."

"Sounds too good to be true," I said, only half listening to Doc. But then I realized that was exactly the behavior I'd seen in Neptune. He'd acted out of character, like someone under the effects of a love drug. And he'd be hurt far worse by rumors of an addiction to HAx5 than by his current fate. I inhaled another puff of oxygen, but this time it did nothing to counter my naturally occurring anxiety. "I've heard it's highly addictive."

"Takes only five hits to make it nearly impossible to shake."

Which meant the need to free Neptune had multiplied, because whoever got to him once only had to get to him four more times.

20: STARDUST

"I THINK I'M OKAY NOW," I SAID TO DOC. I hopped down from the table and set the oxygen canister where I'd been sitting.

"Where do you think you're going?"

"To my room. I have to get my helmet so I can —um—I have things to do. Important uniform business and stuff." I went the door and held my ID card up to the scanner. The door didn't open.

"Sit down," Doc said.

I ran my ID card over the fabric on my catsuit and then held it up again. Again, nothing happened.

"You are my patient. I coded your ID card into the Medi-Bay system, rendering it ineffective. The only way you're getting to the uniform ward is if I accompany you there, and until I determine you're healthy enough to do your job, you're going to stay right here."

"Doc—"

Doc put his hand on my upper arm and steered me back to the table. "Outside this room, you work for the Moon Unit Corporation and follow the commands of the captain. In here, the captain's commands don't mean squat. Until I recode your status, you're my guest. You look awful. You need sleep. You might as well get comfortable."

Doc, unlike the other members of the Moon Unit staff, wasn't particularly fond of Neptune. The two of them had had run-ins in the past, usually ending in hostility. Doc had access to drugs of all kinds and could have easily slipped Neptune something mind-altering. I wanted to trust Doc, but I had to be sure.

"You're the boss," I said blithely. I pulled each shoe off and tossed them into the corner of the room and then hopped back up on the table. "To be honest, I've been working too hard, and I could use a break. You don't mind if I close my eyes, do you?" I faked a yawn. "I'm sort of tired."

Doc cocked his head and studied me from a distance. After a few seconds, he nodded.

"Exhaustion is a common side effect of your system processing unfamiliar chemical compounds. You're in a weakened state. I've got some notes to record. Relax. I'll be at my desk in the back room. I'll check on you in a moment."

I reclined on the table and closed my eyes. I was too keyed up to sleep. I listened to Doc move around and then heard the doors at the back of Medi-Bay swish open and closed. I counted to ten and then twenty to be safe. When it seemed as though Doc was safely preoccupied with his workload, I got up.

Zeke, if he was still in the area, was probably burning up fuel doing laps of the Moon Unit, waiting for me to signal him. Pika was likely passed out from a sugar coma. And Neptune was either drugged again or falling in love with the next person to enter his frame. I didn't even want to think about the condition of the uniform ward. The laundry basket was probably overflowing, and I'd bet the closet was a mess.

My time training at Space Academy, followed with private lessons on security detail and galactic safety, taught me the importance of discovering the immediate concern of any tactical situation. Once that concern was revealed, you pushed all other distraction out of your mind and worked out a solution.

This was often the mistake of the enemy: taking on too much, splitting focus between what they want to achieve and who is trying to keep them from achieving it. In training, we spent days practicing focus. Days of being bombarded with distractions, competitors, threats, pleas, incentives, wants, and desires. It all boiled down to this: find the one thing you want more than anything else, the one thing that you can do given your current circumstances, and throw yourself into it one hundred percent.

Not ninety-nine.

One hundred.

Because what most people didn't understand was that it was easier to give one hundred percent of your focus to a task than to give ninety-nine.

There were so many possible things for me to do that I ran the risk of not doing any. So, I did the one thing I could given the circumstances. I hacked into Doc's computer and searched his recent files to find something incriminating.

And there it was, in a file hidden in a subdirectory called HAx5 Opportunity. I opened it. Inside were notes on the effect of the drug along with clinical trials Doc had conducted over the past year. Patients labeled A–Q had been given varying levels of the drug and observed. Doc's findings were recorded in the subsequent pages, like a journal of medical intel.

It stood to reason that a medical professional—heck, probably all medical professionals—had been tasked to find out a way to cure the effect of a HAx5 overdose. And Doc had an even greater incentive: private donor money. If the Moon Unit owners could lay claim to the cure for the dependency on a highly addictive drug that made the world more beautiful, they could monetize that.

Right now, the most mind-bending substance on the ship was the liqueur in The Space Bar, and even that was diluted for safety. No cruise ship in the galaxy could administer hallucinogens without risk, but imagine if they could. The family-friendly model had quickly been usurped by competitors. This would open up a whole new market.

Forget clearing Doc's debts. This would make him rich beyond his wildest dreams.

I created a link to the computer file and posted it on the dark web with a security code for Zeke. I added a note: *Temporarily detained. Intel enclosed.*

I closed the file and searched for "Neptune."

There were no files on him. I searched on "prisoners," "Cosmos Corsair," and "Federation Council." I added "diabolical plot" and "take this company down" for good measure. Doc appeared to be clean.

As I was about to close the search window, a new file popped up on the computer. It was dated with today's date and time-stamped with the current time. It had to be what Doc was working on in the back room.

I tiptoed toward the back of the room and pressed my ear against the door. I heard the sound of fingers typing on a keyboard. Every time I'd ever seen Doc record notes, he dictated them. This time he typed. It wasn't a suspicious act on its own, but coupled with everything else, it made me wonder what he was up to back there. I went to his computer and opened the file.

It was worse than I expected.

Doc wasn't typing up medical notes about patients he'd seen. He'd been conducting a post-mortem examination. From his back room on the Moon Unit. Which meant there was a dead body on board the ship.

But it wasn't any dead body. It was the one

body that a part of me hadn't believed was dead because no one had seen it.

Doc was conducting the autopsy of Cosmos Corsair.

The doors between Doc and me swished open. "Sylvia? What are you doing?"

I powered down the computer, losing access to his network. I backed away from him until I was up against the tall aluminum refrigeration chamber where he kept the tools he used for operations. He reached the computer and saw the blank screen. "What were you doing?"

"You're performing an autopsy on Cosmos Corsair? You have his body here on the Moon Unit? Does Captain Major Tom know? Who are you working for?"

"Now would be a good time," he said.

"A good time for what?" I pushed past him and into the back room. A lifeless body lay on a long, metal table, eerily illuminated by an overhead neon light. The smell of death overwhelmed me and I turned away—but not before confirming the one fact I needed to confirm.

The body belonged to Corsair.

"You're in violation of a hundred different laws," I said.

"I said now," Doc said again.

"Now what? I didn't ask anything about now."

"Now, damnit!"

And then I felt something I'd never felt before. Tingling in the middle of my body, like a million insects were released and trying to get out through my skin. I glanced down at my hand. It was bright, not the purple I usually turned when I got hot or excited, but magenta, sparkling like I'd had a coating of glitter paint applied to my skin. And in the center of my hand was a white light that traveled up my wrist, past my elbow, and into my upper arm. I lost sight of the glow in my arm but noticed it radiating through my torso. What the—

And then a whoosh of heat and cold, electrons and particles and mass split me apart into a billion specs of energy, and then there was nothing.

21: LIFE ON MARS

"What—how—did I—what a rush!" I exclaimed.

I sat in the passenger seat of Zeke's dad's repair pod. Zeke sat in the pilot seat in front of me. His seat had a swivel feature, and he faced me while the space pod idled in a cluster of stardust that floated in an otherwise Vantablack sky.

"What's your name?" Zeke asked.

"What is wrong with you? It's me. Sylvia." I pulled the hood off my catsuit, revealing my whole head. "Are you okay?"

"I'm fine. You're the one who rematerialized after being broken apart into pieces of energy."

"Is that what that was? Wow!" I'd never known another person or alien to go through a dematerializer, and here I was, having lived to tell the tale! I held my hands out and inspected them. The color of my skin had returned to its usual shade of lavender. "Hold up. How did Ofra dematerialize me? I wasn't in the transport room."

"Doc sent him your coordinates."

"Doc? Doc!" Recent findings flooded back to me. "He's got Cosmos Corsair's body on the Moon Unit."

The news took Zeke by surprise. He forgot to course-correct the repair pod and we flew in a tight corkscrew pattern. I braced myself with both arms and squeezed my eyes shut. I normally had no trouble on a space flight, but the materializer had left me queasy.

After Zeke leveled us out, he turned on the autopilot and faced me. "Doc has Cosmos Corsair? You know this?"

"I know this. I saw the autopsy notes and I saw the body."

"If Doc has the body, then he has to be working with someone. Any idea who?"

"No," I said. "Doc has a network I don't know how to track. There's no telling who he's working with."

I wanted to talk but as the adrenaline rush

wore off, exhaustion hit. Chalk it up to too many dueling medications or a lack of oxygen or the experience of being blown apart and reassembled, but I needed to sleep. Zeke swiveled his seat around and navigated us out into the dark, starless sky, and I sat back and closed my eyes.

"WE'RE HERE," ZEKE SAID.

I opened my eyes. It took a moment to realize I'd fallen asleep, and another couple of moments to figure out why I was wearing a torn black sequined catsuit in the back seat of Zeke's repair pod, how I'd gotten there, and what we were about to attempt. I felt neither calm nor anxious. I'd been on an emotional rollercoaster for the past twenty-four hours and I wondered if this was my new normal.

I looked out the curved Plexiglass window. Wherever it was that we'd arrived, it was dusty and dark. Red lights illuminated the immediate surroundings, casting an eerie glow on the plant life. Plant life?

"Where are we?" I asked.

"One of Mars's moons. You sacked out. I thought Plunians didn't sleep. Did you take something?" He reached his hand forward and used his thumb and index finger to open my eye wide.

I slapped his hand away. "Maybe it's an aftereffect of rematerializing." I didn't want to tell Zeke about the foreign substances swirling through my bloodstream. For someone who maintained a relatively healthy physique and lifestyle, in the past twelve hours, I'd metabolized a whole slew of chemicals. The thought made me feel icky.

Zeke handed me a canister of oxygen connected to a breathing tube. I put the tube into my mouth and secured the canister to my thigh with the attached Velcro straps. Zeke did the same.

Three tall, thin, green men came out of a cave-like structure and walked toward us. The top of the repair pod released and retracted. I slapped Zeke and pointed at the men. He smiled (as best as he could with an oxygen-tank mouthpiece between his lips) and climbed out.

"You must be Zeke and Sylvia," the man in front said.

Zeke pulled his mouthpiece out. "And you must be Ronson." They held their hands up in greeting. Zeke repeated the gesture to the other two men. "Don't mind Sylvia. She's still recovering from her first rematerialization."

Ronson nodded. "Sylvia Stryker. Daughter of Jack Stryker. Colleague of Neptune. Friend of Pika. Savior of Gremlons. Manager of uniforms."

"You have the benefit of knowing who I am and why I'm here. I barely know that."

"You're on Phobos, the closest moon to Mars. We're the SPIDERs." He used his hand to gesture toward the surroundings and the other two Martians. "Woody. Bolder."

The two other Martians held their hands up in greeting.

"Phobos," I repeated. I glanced around at the desolate landscape. I had a flashback to an earlier conversation with the woman from Federal Bureau of Affairs. "This is where Federation Council sends addicts for treatment, isn't it?"

"They used to," he said. "The detention center was destroyed after an accident in the chemical lab." Ronson shoved his hands deep into his pockets. "Follow me."

It was unusual to see a tall, lean Martian. They were called little green men for a reason. But Ronson and the other SPIDERs were head and shoulders above me, with hair that had grown long on top but was shaved on the side. Their clothes were rags, faded fabrics knotted together to create makeshift coverings.

The group of us walked toward the cave. Along the way, I turned my head left and right and marveled at patches of growing foliage. "How'd you grow the plants?"

"You ever hear of red-light therapy?" Ronson asked. I shook my head. "Red lights emit a low-level wavelength to help with photosynthesis. The lights also counter anxiety and bone-density issues caused by traveling through space."

"Does the public know about it?"

"There *may* be people out there who want to regulate the red-light districts," he said. He winked. "We're an under-the-radar operation. Rumor has it you can keep a secret."

"I'm an expert at secrets."

"Right on." He held out a fist, and I bumped it.

We reached the entrance to the cave. Ronson said something to the other two men, who splintered off and headed to the repair pod. "Better not to keep that out in the open. We may be under the radar, but you two will bring us some unwanted attention. Are you hungry? Woody made a vat of Jupiter Jambalaya."

"Sure," Zeke said.

Ronson turned and headed into the cave. I grabbed Zeke's arm and pulled him toward me. "What are you doing? We don't have time to sit around and eat."

"Bring Sylvia a bowl, too, would ya?" Zeke called to Ronson's back.

"You got it." Ronson disappeared.

"Talk," I said. "Who, what, where, when, why. I want it all."

Zeke sat down and put his feet up on the table in front of him. It appeared to be half of a coarse rock, wedged between piles of smaller rocks. Footprints in the dusty moon surface left tracks to the back of the cave. It was clear we were in a highly trafficked area.

"I was running out of fuel doing laps around the Moon Unit. Where were you?" He waved his hand. "Never mind. I know where you were. I didn't know it when I was out there. Ofra received a communication from Doc that you were stuck in Medi-Bay. Seems somebody on the Moon Unit found out that you were sniffing around Neptune's situation and wants you out of the picture."

"Doc may have wanted to me out of the picture because he's involved."

"Either way, Doc's the one who saved you. When he got you to Medi-Bay, he reprogrammed your ID so you were quarantined. Nobody could get to you, and nobody knows you're gone. He sent your coordinates to Ofra, who dematerialized you by remote access and rematerialized you in my repair pod."

"That sounds complicated."

"In the hands of a less-skilled pilot, you'd be mingling with the antimatter right now." He blew on his fingernails and buffed them against the front of his shirt. "Doc's on our side. He's trying to find a treatment for HAx5 overdose. He's been working with Neptune from within the prison."

"Doc and Neptune don't even like each other."

"That's why it was the perfect cover. They were sharing intel. It was the only way the two of them could communicate."

I crossed my arms. I was colder than usual. I missed my prototype uniform. I missed my bubble helmet. I glanced at Zeke's dust-colored clothes, their mismatched shades of outer space dirt intended to blend in with the background and hide any stains he might pick up along the way. He noticed my stare. "Geez! In all the fuss, I forgot about your clothes. Wait here." He jumped up and ran in the direction of where the other two SPIDERs had taken his repair pod.

I stood. All factors indicated I wasn't in any danger, but I liked to figure these things out for myself.

In addition to the chairs and table inside the cave, I found a rock formation that was suspiciously different from the rest of the interior. I slid my hands over the surface and found a small indent in the rocks. It took a few moments to press, pull, tug, and shift the space before it slid aside and revealed a screen and a keyboard. I punched a universal code into the keyboard and then hacked past the firewall to the dark web. Even underground SPIDERs operating from a red-light district on one of Mars's moons were vulnerable.

Martians had an antagonistic relationship with Plunians, and I needed more than Zeke's reassurance that this trio was on the up and up. I navigated to their recent files and discovered a folder that demanded my attention: Cosmos Corsair Murder. I expanded the folder and found a subdirectory that left my blood cold. How To, Timeline, Coverup, Suspects.

I clicked the Suspects folder and found one name: Neptune.

I opened the file and scanned the contents. It was all there: Neptune's means, motive, and opportunity. The details spelled out how Neptune would have gone about killing a prisoner and both when and why he would have done it. It read like a security report filed to Federation Council: dry, emotionless facts that made a case for Neptune's permanent incarceration.

These guys weren't going to help us prove Neptune had been framed. They were going to help put him away for good.

"Exactly what do you think you're doing?" a voice asked behind me.

I turned around slowly and found myself face-to-face with Ronson. In one hand he held a bowl of food, and in the other, he held a phaser.

22: ALAS, INSANE

"Step away from the computer," Ronson said. He set the bowl of jambalaya down and gestured with the phaser.

"What are you going to do with us?" A new fear crept in. "Where's Zeke? Did you kill him already?"

"Geez, Sylvia, calm down. I was getting something to drink." Zeke reentered the cave, holding a tall, narrow glass filled with a ruby-colored beverage in one hand and a duffel bag in the other. A giant straw stuck out the top of his glass. He sucked half the beverage out of the glass, swallowed, and belched. "You guys make a mean spritzer."

"Zeke," I said. "Don't trust them."

"What are you talking about?" he asked. He tossed the duffel bag in my direction, and it landed by my feet. He walked over to Ronson and picked the jambalaya up from where Ronson set it. He carried the bowl and the beverage back to his seat, put his feet up on the table again, and ate calmly, like seeing me held at phaserpoint was the most natural thing in the world.

"Zeke . . ."

"What? Oh, yeah. I forgot." He stood up and carried his bowl to Ronson. The tall, skinny Martian aimed the phaser at the bowl and fired. Steam rose from the bowl. Zeke took another bite. "Thanks, man. Much better."

Ronson set the phaser down on the table. "Hope that didn't scare you," he said. "We use the gun to heat up our food. The natural climate on Phobos makes food to cool down quickly. You live here long enough, you get used to the taste of cold food. I forgot you guys aren't used to it."

"I don't want to talk about food. Why are you framing Neptune for the murder in the space prison? He didn't do it."

"Of course, he didn't do it," Zeke said. "Are you feeling okay, Syl? Is insanity an aftereffect of the rematerializer?"

"You found the file," Ronson said.

"I found the file," I confirmed.

"What file?" Zeke asked.

"He has a file on the murder of Corsair hidden in the protected portion of that computer," I said, pointing at the console. "Inside, there's a file on Neptune that details everything needed to put him away. I don't know what they plan to do with it, but it's clearly incriminating—"

"Oh, that file." Zeke took another bite.

"You know about it?"

"Of course, I know about it. I hacked into their files while I was waiting for you to leave the Moon Unit." He set the bowl and spork down. "Did you actually think I'd fly us out here to ask for help with a mission that holds the life of Neptune in the balance on the basis of Pika's word?"

"How is Pika, anyway?" Ronson asked. His demeanor softened, and I saw real affection in his eyes. It could have been a trick.

"Don't change the subject," I said. I turned back to Zeke. "These guys are Martians. You know how I feel about Martians. You want to trust them, go ahead. Not me."

"They're renegade Martians, which means they're a whole different breed from the rule-following Martians you know. They live on a Martian moon, not on Mars proper. They survived the accident at the detention center when almost everybody else died—"

"Doesn't that seem suspicious? The survival rate was low, but the three of them survived. Maybe *they* blew up the detention center. Did you consider that?"

"For what? They dedicated their lives to helping prisoners. These guys are legit."

"They're framing Neptune." I couldn't believe Zeke was willing to trust them so easily.

"What do you know about Martians?" he asked.

"Aside from the fact that some of the worst moments of my career with Moon Unit Corporation were because of them?"

"Let me put it this way: What are Martians skilled at? What jobs do they often hold?"

"Communications."

"That's right. They have a natural inclination toward languages, dialects, translation, and code breaking. These guys are no different. That file?" He pointed at the console. "They didn't write it. They hacked it from the dark web. Someone else wrote it. Someone who has a vested interest in letting Neptune take the fall for that murder. The SPIDERs are trying to find out who."

"So are we."

"That's right. You already said this was a party-of-five kind of job." He pointed back and forth between us. "One and two." He pointed toward the SPIDERs. "Three, four, five. We'll have more success if we work together."

"You're always like this. Wanting me to work with others."

"You can't save Neptune by yourself, Syl. It's up to you how much time you waste proving I'm right."

Zeke had a point. I'd been isolated for much of my life, and that isolation fed an unhealthy need for control. I trained, practiced, studied, and negotiated my way into any situation knowing I could take care of myself. Most of the time, I could. But this wasn't about me. It was about someone I cared about, someone who'd been there to cover for me when my skills weren't enough.

"Okay, we're here. What do we do next?"

"We listen to what Ronson has to say."

I wasn't entirely thrilled with the idea of letting someone else dictate our plan, but I'd been through too much to get here not to listen. "Let's go."

"You go. I want to check out their data system. I wrote a new nonlinear crypto-algorithm while I was waiting for you to get off the Moon Unit, and they're the perfect candidates to test it for me."

"Be careful."

Zeke grinned. "If I wanted to live a careful life, I wouldn't have ignored my mom's request to clean out the garbage disposal. Remember that the next time you doubt me." He pointed at the duffel bag. "You can thank me for that later."

Zeke left. I opened the bag and found a bubble helmet and a dirt-colored uniform with "CHAMPION" on the back. It was what Zeke and his dad wore when repairing spaceships. It lacked the bells and whistles of my prototype Century 21 uniforms, but it was far more appropriate than the black sequined one I'd been wearing (and had torn) in the past few hours. I slipped it on over my catsuit, fastened the closures, threaded my oxygen tube into my helmet, and breathed.

I followed Ronson deeper into the cave. Once we passed the space where we'd initially congregated, I realized the "cave" was an illusion. Inside, was a massive communication center, with terminals, screens, databanks, and galactic position–system monitors. I studied the GPS monitors and identified the Moon Unit, which moved almost imperceptibly across the screen toward Mars.

"The ship is on its way," I said. "The clock is ticking."

"Let's get on it, then, shall we?"

IT DIDN'T TAKE LONG TO REALIZE RONSON AND company were on our side. The file on Neptune came encrypted with an IP address that traced back to Federation Council's internal communication system. I read over the notes they'd accumulated three separate times before asking the obvious question. "How did you get these?"

"We canvassed the dark web for intel related to Neptune."

"This came from a Federation Council computer. You can't hack into those computers." I said. This, I knew from experience. "Not from the outside, you can't," I added. And then it hit me. "Pika."

Ronson looked away, and I knew I was right. I bit my lip to stay quiet. I wanted to hear him defend himself against my accusation, though his silence confirmed my suspicion.

"I didn't use her," he said.

"If you stole her login credentials or accessed the Federation Council communications database from her computer, then you did. Pika is one of the sweetest aliens I know. She's smart for a Gremlon, but she's still too trusting for her own good. You took advantage of that."

"I didn't take advantage of Pika. She took advantage of me."

"How?"

"She told me she thought something bad was taking place at Federation Council and asked me to look at their files. She gave me her access codes knowing full well what I was going to do."

"But her boss is Vaan Marshall," I said. "If he found out, there would be repercussions."

"That's right." Ronson pointed at the screen where the file on Neptune was displayed. "He did find out, and he cooperated with us. That file came from his computer. Vaan's as interested in finding out who's guilty as you are."

23: SOUL LOVE

"Why would Vaan want to help Neptune?" I asked.

"You tell me," Ronson replied.

A warm flush crawled up my skin. To cover for it, I bent my head down and took a hit of oxygen. I could think of one reason Vaan would want to be involved. It had nothing to do with justice and everything to do with love. If Vaan relaxed his code of ethics to provide us with the information that would lead to Neptune's freedom, I'd spend the rest of my life in his debt.

I felt a buzz on my left wrist and looked down. My communicator lit with an incoming call from Colony 1.

I turned my back on Ronson and tapped the

preview button. It was Angie. Her spiky blond hair stood on end. Her eyebrows were lowered over her eyes and her dark red lips scowled. I raised the communicator and hit Answer. "Century 21 Uniforms, Sylvia Stryker here."

"That's slightly better, but there's room for improvement." Angie said. She squinted. "Where are you? And what are you wearing?"

I shifted my arm so the communication device camera only caught my head. "I loaned my uniform to a prospective client so she could see how it fit."

"You're on a sales call?"

"Yes." I glanced over my shoulder at Ronson and Zeke. Ronson was dressed in tatters. The other two SPIDERs were in similar rags. None of them looked particularly concerned about their outfits, and, frankly, neither was I.

"Where's this sales call? The communicator says you're out of range."

"I'm on Phobos."

"There's only lowlifes and outcasts on Phobos. Nobody worth selling uniforms to. You've got to think big."

"Angie, I'm in the middle of something, and I don't have time to discuss this right now."

Even on the small screen on my wrist, I could

make out Angie pointing her finger at me. "I need results, Sylvia. Orders. Did you talk to the buyer for the Moon Unit?"

"Not yet. I've been focused on the prison."

"I told you, forget the prison. The next time I hear from you, I want good news." She severed the connection.

Did I care about my sales quota? No. But did I like having a cover story, use of a space pod, and an unlimited supply of prototype uniforms? Yes. If I hadn't had a sample garment to send to Lita, I wouldn't have a listening device at my disposal. Which reminded me . . .

I turned around, expecting Ronson to still be there. He wasn't. I followed the sounds of conversation and found all three SPIDERs plus Zeke crowded around a server farm. I left them and walked to the far side of the cave, radioed the Federation Council prison, and asked for Laundry Services. Lita answered the call. "Federation Laundry," she said.

"This is Sylvia Stryker from Century 21 Uniforms. I wanted to follow up on the sample I sent."

"It arrived late yesterday."

"And you've worn it?" It seemed the logical

next thing to say, though I already knew the answer.

"Yes. It's great. I convinced the supply manager to place our next order with you."

"My boss will be happy to hear that. I'll prioritize the order as soon as you send it in."

"I already sent it in," she said. "Didn't she tell you?"

"Who?"

"Your boss. Angie Anderson. She's at the prison all the time, but I didn't put two and two together until this morning."

This morning? "When did you see Angie?"

"Today."

I felt hot and cold at the same time. Angie had dissuaded me from following up with FC as a lead for business, but she'd taken that order herself. And not told me! If she didn't own the company, I would have accused her of being unprofessional.

But something else struck me. "Did you say she's at the prison all the time?"

"Yes. She comes regularly to entertain the prisoners. Sings some of her hits. It was arranged by an advocacy group."

I turned back around and stared at the group clustered by the server. "The SPIDERs?"

"Yes. They do a lot for the prisoners," she said.

I didn't answer right away. I knew Ronson had been at the prison when Corsair was murdered, and now I knew Angie was no stranger to the prison too. My allies were suspects, and my suspects were snitches. There were more possible murder plots to this case than legs on a spider (the regular kind.)

"Sorry about the sales call," I said. I hit disconnect before she could say anything else.

I stormed back to the group. Ronson broke away and met me halfway.

"What is your role at the FC prison?" I demanded.

"We advocate for prisoner rights. Better food, better conditions, better entertainment."

"What about the prisoners who don't deserve to be there?"

"We want the same thing, Lt. Stryker. You want Neptune out. So do we."

"You said Vaan gave you access to his computer. Why would he do that?"

"I have a theory, but it doesn't matter if I'm right. Our mission is to intercept the Moon Unit and extract Neptune. That mission is going to happen with or without you, and if my theory is correct, your involvement might make things more difficult for us."

"But I know things," I said.

"You don't understand why you're here, do you?"

"I'm here to help with your mission."

"No, you're here to stay out of our way. You've got the run of Phobos while we do what we set out to do, but if you interfere, you could compromise everything."

"Does Zeke know that's why I'm here?"

Ronson shook his head. "One of the guys programmed a data leak into our computer. Once Zeke discovers it, he'll be busy for hours trying to figure out where the data is going, who hacked in, how much info we lost."

"Busy work."

"Yes."

"And me?" I crossed my arms. "What did you plan for me to do while I was here? I mean, you went to all that trouble establishing a data breach for Zeke. I'll be offended if you expected me to tend house and wash your dirty dishes." Sarcasm dripped from my tone, and I didn't do a darn thing to hide it. We'd been trapped by a team of

SPIDERs, lured to their web, and then caught, our hands tied so we couldn't help ourselves.

"I did have something planned for you. I think you'll like it." Ronson glided his open palm over a large ball-like device on the desk. A rotation of folders displayed on the screen. He navigated through them until he reached the last one. It was titled "Open Investigation." He stood back, making room for me to take over the keyboard.

"Cut the act," I said. "What am I going to investigate?"

"The same thing you've been investigating all along. The murder of Cosmos Corsair."

"But you said—"

"I said you weren't coming with us on our mission to keep Neptune from reaching Mars. I never said anything about finding out who committed the crime."

"They go hand in hand."

"That's where you're wrong. We don't care who killed Corsair. He was going to die in prison, and he died in prison. The SPIDERs had no reason to rescue him or to advocate on his behalf. We have strong suspicions that Neptune didn't commit the crime, but it would be a waste of our resources to find who did. Even if we did, there's a chance that crime would be covered up, and Neptune's fate wouldn't change. This file is everything we found that could help you discover the real criminal. Based on what Pika told me about you, I thought you'd like it."

"I don't get it. Why give me this info? Why help me figure this out at all? What makes you think I won't use it to design a counter-mission to compete with yours?"

"I know you can't turn your back on this without seeing what's in there. And we need a head start. I password protected the file and buried it behind seventeen firewalls. By the time you access the data, we'll be done."

There was a reason I didn't trust Martians. They were sneaky, and they knew how to do Things. Things like creating seventeen firewalls to hide files that would be imminently useful in conducting a black ops mission. The worst of it was that Ronson knew it would still take less time to hack out the data than to try to find it out for myself.

I hated being so predictable.

24: GETTING ZIGGY WITH IT

THE FIRST ELEVEN FIREWALLS WERE EASY. BY the time I reached the twelfth, I'd developed a false sense of confidence. Who cared how many there were if they were that easy to get past? The twelfth one stopped me dead. After exhausting every hacking protocol I knew, I left the console and headed outside to find Zeke. I found him behind a row of servers in a different part of the cave.

"Don't interrupt me," he said. "I've almost figured this out."

"No, you haven't. You're not going to. It's a trap."

"One more second—"

"Zeke."

"Darn it, Sylvia! Now I have to start over." He

set his dad's diagnostic device on the ground, rolled over onto all fours, and pushed himself up to a standing position. "Do you have any idea how much time I've spent already?"

"Too much. That's what they wanted."

"Who?"

"The SPIDERs. They created the data breach to keep you busy. They buried all the intel I need to solve Corsair's murder behind seventeen firewalls. They know our skill sets, and they tailored these challenges to the things that would keep us occupied while they got a head start."

"On what?"

"Kidnapping Neptune, I think." At Zeke's expression of disbelief, I continued, "I don't think they have malicious intentions. The opposite, actually. But Ronson told me their goal is to intercept his transport and extract him."

"That's good, right?"

"That's bad. He'll be a fugitive. For the rest of his life. No jobs on Moon Unit, no teaching at Space Academy, no freelancing. Neptune will have to disappear. He won't even be able to resume life on the Kuiper Belt." (At least, thanks to my smart off-planet investments, he'd have a start-up fund.)

"That would be a problem for him. It'll be a problem for you too."

"Don't worry about me. I can visit him without anybody knowing."

"You don't get it, do you? You and Neptune aren't mentor and mentee. You're not friends. You lost everything recently, but you found him. He challenges you; I see it. And you challenge him. You guys are good for each other, or you would be if you'd get over your whole military/security-training/who's-better-at-their-job thing."

"If Neptune would acknowledge I'm better, that would all go away."

"Sylvia..."

"You know you're the best hacker in the galaxy, right? How come you don't have to acknowledge someone else out there might be as good as you?"

"Because nobody is."

"See? That. How come I have to concede? Why can't I be the best at what I do? Is it because I'm a girl?"

"Get over yourself! That boy/girl stuff only exists on Earth. You're great at what you do. Your reputation proceeds you. You even told me Neptune heard about you before he was scheduled to teach at the academy. But consider this: if you're the best, and Neptune is the best, imagine how great you two could be if you joined forces."

"I don't see you joining forces with anybody."

"I'm in business with my dad. When he retires, I'll take over his route. There are enough jobs out there to keep me rolling in more crypto-currency than I could spend in ten lifetimes." Zeke's expression changed to one of apology. "Speaking of which, my dad said no to the new uniforms."

"Doesn't matter," I said. I wanted to keep talking to Zeke, but this conversation was as much of a distraction as the tasks the SPIDERs had prepared for us. That was when I realized how easily we'd been tricked. It wasn't a matter of knowing our skill sets and giving us individual challenges. It was making us compete with ourselves to prove something we both already knew.

"We're wasting our time. Come with me."

"Give me two more minutes to figure out this data breach."

I turned away from Zeke and did a slow three-sixty. The SPIDERs powered their facilities somehow, and we had to find the source. I turned back to Zeke. "Where's the repair pod?"

"Outside the cave, behind a rock formation."

"Come on." I grabbed his arm and pulled him away from the server. "I have an idea."

We raced to the space pod. Zeke fired it up, and I pointed above us. "Go up. Straight up." He did. When we hovered two hundred feet above the cave, I said, "Flip us slowly. I need to see directly below us."

Zeke didn't ask questions. He flipped the space pod. He zigged and he zagged, maneuvering the vehicle over the SPIDERs' compound while I searched for something to indicate their power source. It had to be there. Somewhere.

And then, I saw it. Zeke did too. The red light beams that I'd noticed upon landing made up a web. I traced them to the epicenter, a glowing spot directly over a cluster of plants that had no business growing on a Martian moon. "There," I said.

Zeke nodded. He piloted the space pod to the spot. As we got lower to the ground, we lost sight of the red lights. "I can't see the grid when we're this low," he said.

"Do you have a cable?"

"Yes."

"Then stay up high. I'm going down."

I attached the cable to my ankle and pressed

the seat-release button. The floor below me opened, and I dropped out.

The gravity on Phobos was weaker than what was maintained in common areas where humans, aliens, and animals comingled. Even with the thrust of falling out of Zeke's space pod, I glided more than dead-dropped down. I detached my oxygen canister from my thigh, took a massive gulp, and then aimed the nozzle away from me toward the ground. When the burst of gas hit the intersecting light beams, they moved, keeping me focused on the point at which I wanted to land.

And land I did. On top of a cabbage patch that wasn't a cabbage patch. It was a fake plant left in place to hide the on/off switch that operated the entire SPIDER power grid. And by landing on it, I effectively switched it off.

The planet surface went dark. We weren't in front of the servers or the computer with the databanks and firewalls, but I knew they were dark too. Anything that required more than a wind turbine was dead to the world. The only light source came from an amber glow in the distance that did little in terms of providing visibility.

Zeke, aware that I'd finished what I'd set out to do, initiated the cable-retraction system. I felt a slight jerk, and then slowly, I was pulled up to the space pod. I straightened out my body, slipped into the same hole through which I'd exited, and settled back into my seat. The bottom of the space pod slid closed, and Zeke pulled back and flew us up and away from the surface of the moon. "Where to now, boss?"

"We have to find out what the SPIDERs know. Ronson said those files contained everything I'd need to know to find out who killed Cosmos Corsair."

"But you said you couldn't access them. The SPIDERs still know more than us, and it doesn't seem like they're going to be forthcoming when we tell them we failed their test."

"We're not going to tell them we failed their test. They gave us everything we need. We weren't paying attention." I couldn't believe I hadn't put it all together before now. I felt particularly duped, and I suspected Zeke would, too, once I told him what I believed. "They had me hacking into a database of info they stole from Federation Council's internal communications network. They had you plugging a data breach. Neither one of us was successful. Do you know what that means?"

"We failed for the first time in our lives?"

"No, we found our way in."

Zeke's temporary confusion gave way to anticipation. "You want me to take you to Federation Council so you can steal the info yourself."

"Yes. And while I'm going through Federation Council files, you can see what's been flowing out of that data breach the SPIDERs were using you to plug."

25: ROCK 'N' ROLL SUICIDE

IT WAS A TURBULENT TRIP TO COLONY 1. ZEKE did his best to negotiate the debris, but we sustained several hits, rocking us this way and rolling us that. The heavy webbing belts that secured us into our seats kept us from bouncing around too much, but I couldn't avoid the notion that even if we arrived safely, we were still on something of a suicide mission.

The drugs Doc had given me had fully metabolized while on Phobos, and I was back to feeling a combination of human emotions—nerves, excitement, adrenaline, fear—with my Plunian rationality. The two had become intertwined, and I couldn't shut one off anymore. My mind was filled with questions and hypotheses about whether I could trust the SPIDERs, whether Ronson had a reason to lie about Vaan, whether we'd given up too soon in the ability tests to which we'd been assigned. Whether there was a data breach or a file of incriminating information.

I didn't need questions. I needed answers. I focused on the facts that I knew, but each fact tugged on newly discovered heartstrings that led back to friends that were at risk of getting hurt. I'd lost some of my edge. It couldn't be helped without taking another form of medication, but I wasn't going to leave the outcome of our mission to mind-altering chemicals.

Fact: Ronson said Pika gave him access to her computer and login credentials to see what was going on.

Fact: Pika trusted Ronson.

Arguable Fact: Ronson was trustworthy.

Fact: Ronson had been at the prison the morning of the murder.

Arguable Fact: Ronson was on an extraction mission to get Neptune.

Conclusion: Ronson didn't have enough intel to prove Neptune didn't commit murder.

What could that mean? Ronson knew Neptune wasn't guilty but couldn't prove it . . . or maybe he could. Maybe he was protecting the real murderer.

Maybe *he* was the real murderer.

That was no good!

What other suspects did I have?

Angie had been on Colony 1 at the time of the murder. She kept warning me away from the prison, though Lita told me Angie was there all the time. Was that significant?

And what about Lita? There was that suspicious conversation I'd lifted from the recording in her uniform. Now that I stopped to think about it, I questioned the way she stumbled into me (and others) on the path. She'd explained it as an ear infection, but that could have been a convenient excuse. Maybe she was on drugs. Maybe her erratic behavior was because she needed a fix.

Lita had kept me chatting about uniforms when I left Federation Bureau of Affairs. If she'd been watching me, that could have been a diversion. Plus, she'd been carrying that prisoner transfer notice. Why would the prison laundress be cc'd on a memo about prisoner transport?

I'd been so caught up chasing details that it didn't matter that I'd lost all sight of questions I should have asked by now: How did Cosmos Corsair die? What was the time of his death? Was that what Doc was trying to figure out with his autopsy?

Doc. I wanted to trust him, but I was afraid to trust anybody. The possession of Corsair's body indicated he was somehow connected to either the prison or the murder or both. What about eliminating the source of so much illness and addiction? As a medical professional, Doc had sworn an oath to heal people, but if given the chance, would he participate in a plot to eliminate Corsair? Could he separate himself from the bad things the pirate had done by leaking his drug into the water supply and infecting thousands of innocents? Or when given the chance, would he act like a man fueled with righteous anger and destroy the root of all evil?

A trained military person would have been able to keep his hatred in check. I didn't know if Doc had that ability. He'd never shown respect to the enforcers that we encountered and sometimes criticized Neptune's ability to follow rules blindly in the face of life-and-death threats.

But could Doc commit murder?

And then there were countless others: the

inmates who served time with Corsair. How many of them had been touched by his network? These were men who'd already committed crimes and incarceration might make them desperate. Was killing someone while you're on the inside that much more of a stretch?

Zeke ducked the ship into a wormhole and popped us out the other side. Seconds later, we careened through the entry point to Colony 1. We were going too fast. We were going to crash. If we crashed, we'd die, which would put a serious damper on our goal of sneaking in without being noticed.

"I have an idea," Zeke said. "You game?"

"Go for it."

He cut the wheel to the left, and the space pod tipped at a dangerous angle. Our velocity pulled us into a vortex of centrifugal force. We slung around the interior of the dome that kept the colony atmosphere protected. Zeke cut the engine.

The ship flew in a wide circle, slowing gradually, until finally, it slipped down the dome and got closer to the ground. He punched several codes into his nav system and released a spray of white foam out of a chamber by the exhaust pipes. By the time we completed one last rotation of the dome, we'd slowed to a safe speed. He aimed the steering controller down, and we nosedived directly into the foam.

"Getting out is going to be messy," I said.

"Not nearly as messy as getting dead."

He released the hatch, and foam oozed in and coated me. I fought against it, finally throwing my legs over the edge of the space pod and dropping to the ground. Zeke shook his head. He pulled a tab next to his seat, and a long yellow chute rolled out and inflated. He dove onto it and glided down, stopping next to my feet. "You miss out on all the fun."

"This isn't the time for fun."

I grabbed his hand and pulled him to his feet. "How well do you know Colony 1?"

"Not very. Federation Council blocked me from working on their ship repairs." He made a face. "It's like they don't trust me."

I was such a fool. "It's because of me, isn't it?" I asked quietly. "You stayed friends with me all along. After my dad was arrested, after the trouble with the Moon Units, after Neptune was arrested, all of it. A lot of people cut ties with me even after Dad was avenged, but you never did. You paid a price for that."

"Don't go soft on me, Syl. I like my freedom, and I get a rush doing things that are against the law. The Federation Council is right not to trust me. Now let's go break into their computer system and catch ourselves a killer."

I threw my arms around him. "You're the best shady space-pod repairman *ever*."

I dusted my arms and legs free of white foam and led the way to Federation Council. Zeke kept a wallet of cloned security keycards from previous jobs, and one of them gave us access to the maintenance building. It wasn't the ideal entry point, but it was something. Before Zeke used the keycard, he turned to me. "Once we're in, we should try to be as quiet as possible. I didn't have a chance to check the security protocols of Federation Council, but I assume they've got more than cameras."

"Infrared motion detectors and sound-level monitors. And there are machines that run atmosphere-disruption diagnostics every ten minutes."

A slow smile crept onto Zeke's face. "How accurate is your info?"

"I've been dreaming about breaking into Federation Council since I was twenty. I update my records of their security protocols with my morning tea."

"You're wasting your time on uniforms," Zeke said. His smile had expanded, and there was no mistaking his enthusiasm. "Any words of advice before we go in?"

"Yes. Try not to be seen."

As soon as I said it, the door opened, and Lita, the prison laundress, grabbed my wrist. "We don't have all day," she said and pulled me inside.

26: UNDER PRESSURE

I STUMBLED MY WAY INTO THE LAUNDRY ROOM. "Shhhhh," Lita whispered. She pushed the door shut behind her.

The locking mechanism clunked into place, and a red light turned on above the door. And Zeke was nowhere to be found. Inside the room was a row of empty bins. Next to them were stacks of neatly folded uniforms still in packaging. I recognized them immediately. They were fresh from the Century 21 Uniform inventory.

It was the order Angie had fulfilled. Proof that Angie had been in contact with the prison. That she'd been in contact with Lita. I didn't know what it meant, but I didn't think it meant anything good.

Lita was wearing the sample uniform I'd messengered to her the day we spoke. It retained its clean appearance thanks to self-sanitizing threads that had been woven into the fabric, though small frays by the seams told me she'd erroneously put it through a laundry cycle.

To my left were cleaning supplies: mops, buckets, chemicals to mix together to disinfect the place. The universe had embraced technological advances in almost every field, but in the area of cleaning, apparently nothing equaled a one-to-one mixture of toxic chemicals and water for killing germs.

This was mostly what I'd expected to find when entering the maintenance wing. The difference was in my daydreams, I didn't have company.

Lita and I stared at each other for longer than was comfortable. The only light came from a bulb over the sanitizing machines along the wall. In the darkness, I couldn't gauge things like her pupil dilation, her increased nervous state, or her receptivity to intimidation tactics. All things considered, she'd set it up so I was at a disadvantage.

"I was staring out the window when your ship

entered the geodome. I saw you circle the perimeter and crash into the foam."

"I'm not going to hurt you," I said. It was unclear whether Lita was going to help me or turn me in, but as long as Zeke was on the outside with a working and nontraceable keycard, there was a chance I'd have a two-against-one situation soon. Besides, I could take her in a fight. I had all sorts of high-level training, and she looked like a cream puff. Banking on that, I continued, "I need access to the your computer so I can check some data points. That's it. I'm not going to disrupt the prison, and I'm not going to break anybody out."

"Yes, you are."

"No—"

Lita was desperate. "My brother is in there," she said. She grabbed my wrists and held me in place. "I took this job so I could keep tabs on him. He's small, and he's easy to pick on. And there's only so much I can do to protect him."

That was when I recognized what it was I'd seen when I ran into her in the quad after filing the report on Neptune's untimely death. It wasn't a drug addiction or a thinly veiled attempt to cover up a crime. It was helplessness.

Here was a woman who took her job to keep

tabs on her brother, but aside from watching him from afar, she couldn't do anything to change his circumstances. My training armed me with the skills to complete my mission, and my determination to see things through meant I'd succeed or die trying. You could say the Federation Council hardwired me to break into their system from the day they turned their backs on me.

"You're the one who removed Neptune's name from the transport paperwork," I said.

Lita looked terrified. "That paperwork—where is it?"

It wasn't a denial, but her fear was unexpected. "You dropped it in the quad the day you ran into me."

"Do you have it?"

"I threw it out."

She bent over, her hands on her face. "That was my last chance," she mumbled from between fingers. Her shoulders shook like she was sobbing, and a whole different explanation of the transport paperwork with the missing name came to me.

"The paperwork was legitimate. You were going to put your brother's name on the paperwork to get him out," I guessed.

She dropped her hands and stood back up. "Garson is a good kid. He shouldn't be in here."

"What's he in for?"

"Grifting."

"Did he do it?"

"I don't know."

It wasn't the worst crime to have committed. Zeke bought his first set of lock-picking tools from running grifts around Space Academy. Lita's brother hadn't seemed to use the money for himself either. My heart went out to her for taking a job to keep watch over him.

"Lita, breaking someone out of jail is its own mission. I'll come back and do what I can when I'm done, but I can't do both. Not now. The SPIDERs put me at a disadvantage—"

"The SPIDERs?" She braced herself with both hands as if the mention of the rescue team made her knees weak. "Are you working with them?"

"They're working on their own to intercept a prisoner transport, and if they're successful, that prisoner will have to live off the grid for the rest of his life."

"They intercepted Neptune," she guessed correctly. "That's why you're here."

"Neptune doesn't belong here either," I said. "He did nothing wrong. I can't let a good man lose his freedom over a crime he didn't commit."

"It's better than being executed," she said.

"It's not a life."

"Neither is this." The words were quiet, as if she'd accepted her fate of working a thankless job because it was all she could do for her brother. "Garson is all I have left," she said. "After the pirates ravaged Pluto, we lost everything."

"You live on Pluto?"

"Lived," she said. "After the pirates destroyed our ecosystem, the government collapsed. Garson was arrested in a sweep of young men who were locked up as a precautionary measure against rioting. I don't even know if the grifting charges were real. The others bought their way out—isn't that the way with corruption?—but we had no money. We accepted a prison sentence in exchange for a roof over our heads. And now that Pluto's for sale, we'll never be able to go back."

I didn't raise her hopes, but I raised my own. Because if Ofra Starr won the bidding war, his third act of Congress was going to be affordable housing for Plutonians—*all* Plutonians—but especially Lita and her brother.

But first things first. I had a government of my own to overthrow.

27: PANIC IN DE PRISON

Lita picked a uniform out of the laundry bin. "Change out of your clothes, and put this on," she said. "It's what the inmates wear, and you'll blend in more."

"I can't blend. I'm purple."

"Trust me," she said. I didn't move. "The visual cameras are infrared. Your skin will look like everybody else." She held the uniform toward me. Our hands brushed against each other's, and she recoiled.

"I run hot," I said.

"This isn't going to work."

"You said—"

"Not because you're purple. The prison is equipped with a Temperature Variance Detector.

If you go in there, the TVD will send a silent alarm to the security team about an intruder. They'll be able to track your movement by isolating your temperature."

"What if I leave my catsuit on under the uniform?"

"That'll make you hotter. We have to cool you down."

There'd been one time in my past when an unfortunate combination of factors left me in an ice bath, and I wasn't rushing to relive the memory. "No," I said quickly. "If my core temperature drops too much, I'm at a disadvantage. I can't think. I can't fight. I need all my skills to work at peak, especially if I'm going to get your brother out too."

Sadness settled onto Lita's shoulders. They dropped from the invisible weight, and the uniform that she'd wanted me to take fell to the floor.

I could do this on my own—or with Zeke, if he managed to get in undetected. And I didn't need to take on an unplanned rescue mission while inside Federation Council.

But did I want to be that kind of security agent? All mission, no heart? How far would I have gotten on this rescue mission if I didn't have unexpected help?

"We can raise the temperature in the prison," I said. "If the differential between the interior temperature and me is within an undetectable range, the Temperature Variance Detector won't detect me, right? You said that's their mechanism for identifying intruders?"

"Yes, but . . . I know!" She turned to the row of laundry-sanitizing machines and quickly spun dials and punched the start buttons. Immediately, the silence was interrupted by the sounds of chugging and whirring. She grabbed a mop and jabbed the handle end at the vents above the machines. "The machines expel hot air into the commissary. That's the room directly behind mine. In ten minutes, it'll be like a steam bath. But it's after hours, so there's no reason to monitor it, and there won't be any movement to set off the alarm. By the time they figure out the problem, you'll already have been through the room and into the delivery halls that lead to the prison."

"And then what?"

"Then you get my brother and bring him back here."

While we waited for the temperature in the commissary to rise enough to mask my presence, I accessed Lita's computer. She wasn't connected to the Federation Council network, but because her job required her to hire independent contractors for the occasional cleaning or uniform needs of the prison, she had access to the outside.

She gave me her login credentials with the expected caution, "Don't get me fired."

The numerous reasons why that mattered went unspoken.

I left Lita to the laundry. She'd already cleaned everything, but to keep up the charade of running the system (thus heating up the commissary), she started over with the exception of one: mine. I changed into the loose-fitting prisoner uniform and stashed Zeke's loaner outfit and my torn-beyond-repair black catsuit behind the laundry bin. At least part of my superhero powers came from the garments I wore, but this time I had to rely on 14-ounce white denim with "PRISONER" stamped on the back.

I sent a communication to Zeke.

You there?

>>>

Requesting space repairman to Federation Council Prison

>>>

Initiating radio silence

>>>

The cursor blinked too many times. Wherever Zeke was, he wasn't at his computer.

I cloned the messaging window and used my Moon Unit login to hack into their internal messaging board. I sent a series of communications to the Moon Unit, to Captain Major Tom, to Pika, and to Ofra. I didn't care who picked up on them, only that someone responded. They included a cry for help and the coordinates to the Federation Council prison.

If someone received the communication acted, I might be saved. But if I got caught, I might as well get used to this uniform because I'd be wearing it for life.

I got through the commissary and entered a crawlspace reserved for food delivery. An archaic rope-and-pulley system operated, with effort, to get me to the third floor. I crawled out and faced the prison cells.

Who were these people? Actual criminals? Or victims like Lita's brother? Had they committed crimes or been the target of an overly eager justice system determined to meet quotas and look effective? I'd agreed to break out one of them, but how many were innocent? How many others deserved their freedom?

The schematics that Lita had saved on her computer indicated the location of the master controls: one that turned off the infrared (don't touch that one!) and one that overrode the lockdown system. Next to the two master controls was a panel with switches that corresponded to every single cell. She'd given me the number of her brother's cell. All I had to do was reach the panel and flip his switch, and my obligation to her was done.

The inmates seemed to sense my presence. Even though I made every effort to be quiet, they were restless. They tossed and turned. Some threw back their covers, and others kicked feet out from underneath. It was the heat. It hadn't occurred to me that the inmates were as much of a threat to my anonymity as the security guards. If they kept this up, one of them would trigger the motion detector and bring on the people I wanted to avoid.

I ran past the cells, no longer worried about going slow to avoid detection. I reached the control panel and gasped. The front panel that contained the corresponding numbers to the prisoner cells had been removed, leaving a cluster of unidentifiable switches and wires exposed.

"Hey!" called out a deep male voice. I whirled around. Four large men in head-to-toe black stormed toward me. They were prison guards, dressed like the men who'd entered the Federation Bureau of Affairs the day I filed the falsified paperwork. "You, by the panel. How'd you get out?"

I forgot about my prisoner uniform. This was bad! It was one thing if they thought I'd broken in with the intent of breaking someone out, but quite another if they suspected I should be locked up myself.

I held up my hands. "It's not what you think," I said. "I'm running a diagnostic analysis of the prison security system. I was told it would be less disruptive to the inmates if I looked like one of them." The lie tumbled out of my mouth. It was the most ridiculous thing I could have made up, but I wasn't thinking clearly.

The men didn't stop their advance. The closer they got, the bigger they looked. Big and mean. I stepped backward. Even with the defensive maneuvers Neptune had taught me, I doubted I could take out four massive security guards. I receded two more steps when I backed into the wall behind me.

Correction: I backed into the button that turned off the infrared light source.

The second the red light turned off, the world was awash in bright, bold colors. There were the blue railing, the gray floor, the white ceilings, and the silver bars on each cell.

And inside the cells were purple faces of inmates staring out at me.

Plunians, more Plunians than I'd been told had survived when our planet exploded. They were locked up like animals in cages. And I knew they'd done nothing wrong. They couldn't have. These were refugees from my home planet who'd been promised housing by the Federation Council and locked up in jail instead.

Rage built up inside me. And at the core of it, I remembered something Neptune had told me when he sacrificed himself: the needs of the many outweigh the needs of the one.

This time I was the one. And I had the ability to fix this.

I turned around and slapped my hand against the other button. The cells opened up, and in the span of seconds, every prisoner who'd been locked up in Federation Council jail was free.

THIS WASN'T A PRISON RIOT. IT WAS pandemonium. As soon as the cells were open, the inmates flooded onto the balcony. The security guards were overwhelmed. Catching me meant nothing compared to containing this outbreak. If even one prisoner made it out, the news would learn who the inmates of Federation Council jail really were.

Questions fought to enter my brain, but I blocked them. I knew something wasn't right, but there wasn't time to reason through it all now. I backed my way to the crawlspace, only to find a young boy already inside.

"Come on," he said. "There isn't time."

"I'm not leaving the prison yet," I said. "You need to go with the others. There's safety in numbers."

"No," he said. His voice was quiet but confident. "I know who you are."

And I knew who he was too. He was a younger, boyish version of Lita. Despite his youth and small physique, he had an air of determination about him. If prison did change a person, then this person had learned to face his fears.

"You're Garson, aren't you?" I asked. He nodded. "I promised your sister I'd get you out. She's waiting for you in the laundry room. You need to meet her there."

"Aren't you coming with me?"

"I can't." I put my hand on his shoulder. "Your goal was to get out. My goal is a little more elaborate. I might not achieve my goal, but you can't let that get in the way of you achieving yours."

Garson looked nervous. "I'm going up," I said, pointing toward to the cavernous passageway over our heads. "There's nothing but trouble up there. Your freedom is two floors down, through the commissary."

And right as Garson seemed to make up his mind to listen to me, the decision was taken out of his hands. The rope pulled upward, carrying both of us deeper into the building.

28: WATCH THAT MAN

THERE WAS NO GETTING OUT OF THE crawlspace and no predicting what (or who) we'd find when the pulley stopped. I took Garson's hand, and he held it so tightly the lavender color by my knuckles turned white. He was shaking, but he didn't break down. I wondered what he'd seen inside the prison that had toughened him up to this point.

"Looks like you're going to help me after all," I said. Immediately I regretted making light of our predicament. I shifted my weight and looked directly at him. "Chances are we're walking into a trap. If you do what I tell you to do, you'll be okay. Can you do that?"

"I think so."

"I mean it. I won't be polite. I won't say 'please' and 'thank you.' I'm going to give you orders, and you have to follow them. You can't ask questions."

"Can I ask a question now?"

I nodded.

"Are we going to die?"

"Not if you do what I say."

The pulley jerked at uneven intervals. Who knew how much time we had? Maybe the person pulling us up was doing so with the intention of letting us fall. The farther the drop, the more likely we wouldn't survive. Risk assessment: there was no risk in telling Garson what I was there to do, because the likelihood of survival and escape was infinitesimal.

"There was a prisoner in here named Neptune," I said.

"I know Neptune. He was my friend."

"He's my friend too. The news says he murdered another prisoner, and the authorities want to move him to Mars."

"Neptune's gone. They already took him."

"I know. And there are people working on that, too, but nobody cares about who committed the crime. The only way to prove Neptune didn't commit murder is to prove who did. That's why I'm here."

If Garson was shaking before, he was darn near vibrating now. For a moment, I feared I was suffering from the same hallucinogens Neptune had before he passed out. I put my hand on Garson's foot and realized the nervous vibration was coming from him. "Stick with me, okay? I won't let anything happen to you."

We jerked to a halt. Garson pulled away from me and pressed himself against the interior wall. The air in the prison had been a high-enough mix of oxygen to keep me from feeling weak, but this tight space was filled with stale air. I'd left my helmet and oxygen tank with Lita, and if I didn't get out, I'd suffocate. I stomped the soles of my shoes against the wall to announce our presence.

A door slid up, revealing an exit. I threw my legs out and turned to help Garson. He shifted closer to me and reached out as I heard a voice behind me. "Sylvia!"

I turned my head. "Zeke?"

Zeke ran toward me and grabbed my hand. "We have to get you out of here. There's been a prison break, and they've initiated lockdown procedures. Did you get what you needed from the computer system?"

"Um—"

It was at that point that Zeke noticed my uniform. "Why are you dressed like an inmate?"

"I ran into some trouble and had to change plans. Did you know Federation Council locked up Plunians? They were told they were getting temporary housing on Colony 1. If this is what the Federation meant by temporary housing, they deserve to be locked up themselves."

"You're behind the prison break, aren't you?"

"We'll talk about that later. Did you find an access point?"

"This way." Zeke got about twenty feet from the crawlspace before he discovered I wasn't with him. I went back to talk to Garson.

"I know you're scared. You can stay here if you want, but you'll be safer with us." I said. Garson didn't move. "I have to keep moving, but I'll send help for you. In the meantime, don't trust anybody. You can trust me, and you can trust him." I pointed at Zeke. "If you see somebody who doesn't look like me or him, then assume they're bad. Got it?"

"Got it," Garson said with fake bravado. I started to leave, and he caught my oversize sleeve and pulled me closer. "I have something for you." He reached under his uniform and pulled out a set of dog tags with a single star embossed on the back.

"Neptune wanted you to have these."

Neptune obviously had been looking out for the kid, and I knew why. Garson was the witness. I didn't believe for a second Neptune would leave him alone in here. But the timeline didn't fit. If Garson saw someone kill Cosmos Corsair, then Neptune wouldn't have had the chance to give him the dog tags. That must have happened before the murder, before Neptune was isolated, before he was transferred to the Moon Unit. Why would Neptune have been protecting this kid before there was a crime?

But there *was* a crime. The Plunians being locked up was a crime. And it confirmed every rumor I'd heard about corruption in Federation Council. It was something my dad had hinted at the last time I saw him. That all the news we saw of the Federation Council protecting the universe was a myth, that deep inside there was more of an interest in power and control than a utilitarian doctrine.

Garson might not have seen the murder of Cosmos Corsair, but I'd be willing to bet he saw something else. And Neptune knew it. And the murder of a prisoner that nobody would have missed was a warning shot to leave it alone. The frame-up got Neptune out of the way, so Garson was left to fend for himself. I wondered if the council even knew Garson's big sister had been looking out for him after his bodyguard had been removed.

I went back to Zeke. "There's a kid in there. He's part of this. You need to get him out of here while I hack into the computer, okay?"

"About that. You're not the only one who did something." Zeke looked over both shoulders. "You know how the SPIDERs programmed that data breach while we were on Phobos?" He rushed ahead, not waiting for me to confirm. "I kept thinking about how risky that was. They opened a backdoor and let data be visible to anybody who had an interest in getting in. You don't do that by accident, and you don't do that to create busywork. They wanted someone to see what they had."

"Did you see what they had?"

"I thought we'd be back on the Moon Unit by now. The computer in your room was a way more sophisticated system than the portable one I have in the space pod. I could have figured that out in record time if I had your RAM."

"How do you know about the computer in my room? It was some sort of requisition error. I'm a second lieutenant. I never should have been given that kind of hardware."

"It was a gift," he said. "I hacked into the Moon Unit database and changed the requirements for the Uniform lieutenant. I upgraded your bed, gave you a fridge filled with your favorite snack foods, and changed your rank to first lieutenant so the ship staff would be more accommodating."

"You did that?"

Zeke shrugged. "I figured if I ever came to visit you, it would be more fun if your room was like a five-star hotel."

I'm not going to lecture him. I'm not going to lecture him. I'm not going to lecture him.

There was a reason Zeke went to work for his dad instead of pursuing a career in the cruise ship industry or going into the military. He liked fun too much. I couldn't fault him, but fun wasn't my default setting. Maybe someday it would be, but right now, there was too much at stake.

"Why are you telling me this now?"

"I couldn't plug the data breach, but I could reroute it to a safe server."

"You sent all that data to my computer on the Moon Unit?"

"I tried to, but your computer is missing from the network. Do you think someone figured out what you're up to? Because it's almost like it's unplugged."

"Pika is in my room. For all I know, she hollowed out the monitor and used it as a bed for Cat." Zeke paled. "You said you found a safe server. Where?"

"There's only one other computer on the Moon Unit that had the capacity for it. It's hardwired to compartmentalize new information without scanning it for classified information. You sent me a file from it yourself."

"The Medi-Bay computer," I correctly guessed.

"Yes. Is that a problem? I figured Doc wouldn't notice."

"Doc's hiding Corsair's body in his back room. He wouldn't have it without the help of Federation Council. If he discovered the data breach, he'd not only notice, but he'd be duty bound to report it to the elders."

"That's exactly what he did," said a new voice. "Good thing I intercepted his report."

I knew that voice. I knew it, and once upon a time, I'd trusted it. Slowly I turned and faced my old lover, confidant, friend, and fellow Plunian. Vaan.

29: NOTHING HAS CHANGED

"This has to stop, Sylvia," Vaan said. "It's gone too far. The Moon Unit Corporation has been nothing but trouble for you. Can't you see it?"

"Right now, I can see a lot of things, but that's not one of them."

"You saw the Plunian inmates," he correctly guessed. "I'm glad you saw them. I'm glad you know. Do you have any idea how hard it is to be a member of the council when I know how corrupt they are?"

"You know?"

"I've known for a long time. After your dad was arrested, I did some digging. I found dubious motives. Payoffs. I tried to bring it up and was told not to make trouble. Shortly after that, Plunia was destroyed. It was as if they were sending me a message."

"Our planet was destroyed by a space pirate. They're a plague on the galaxy, and the Federation Council is supposed to be doing something about them."

"And they have. The worst of the pirates have been locked up or killed. I don't like what Neptune did, but I'm not going to pretend I care about Cosmos Corsair."

"You still believe Neptune killed him? Even after you admitted to knowing about the corruption here?"

"It wouldn't be the first pirate Neptune killed," Vaan said. "I don't like his methods, but I admire his results."

"And it doesn't bother you that he's being moved to Mars? That he's going to be left to work out his days on a chain gang?"

"Even if Neptune doesn't do anything else in his life, he'll be a legend for all the good he's done so far."

"That's not right, and you know it."

"It's his life, Syl. It doesn't have to be yours." Vaan approached me and ran his fingers over my hair. I studied his face. He was bald like Neptune, but the similarity between the two men ended there. Neptune had sex appeal that caused a physiological reaction in me when we were in the same room. Vaan's presence made me calm. With Neptune, I never knew what he thought of me. Vaan hadn't tried to keep his feelings secret. The two of them represented danger versus safety, uncertainty versus security. Heat versus cool. Lust versus love.

But I'd learned enough to know none of these emotions existed in a vacuum. I'd felt more danger in Neptune's presence than I'd known in my life, but I'd also felt more alive. And while I may never get a grand proclamation of love from him (that wasn't influenced by HAx5), I knew to my core he'd protect me.

"I need to see your computer," I said. "It's why I came, and I won't leave until it's done."

"What do you expect to find?"

"Nothing, I hope." And I believed that to be true.

Vaan stepped away from the desk. "Go ahead," he said.

The morning I tried to have Neptune declared dead was also the last morning I'd talked to Vaan about the situation. There had been something suspicious about his reaction, and I hadn't spent a lot of time examining that other than to chalk it up to jealousy. But now, here he was, cooperating with me despite his standing in the Federation Council.

Vaan had been by-the-book since graduation, and getting this position cemented that. It was why we'd butted heads during past altercations and why I knew we'd never be compatible long-term. I hadn't expected him to step aside and give me access to his files. I'd gone to great lengths with Zeke to be able to hack into them. Had Vaan changed? Had I underestimated his desire to do good?

I slid into his seat. The screen was an overly bright shade of blue that hurt my eyes. I blinked twice and looked away. "Use these," Vaan said. He handed me a pair of blue-light glasses. "The Federation Council monitors are calibrated for human eyes, not Plunian ones. The lenses will counter the effect."

I slipped on the glasses and looked at the screen again. The painfully harsh shades of blue were muted to dull shades of gray. A Federation Council logo rotated on the center of the screen. I clicked the logo and pulled up the subdirectory. Vaan stood in front of the computer, watching my face while I watched the screen. It bolstered my confidence in both him and in my hacking abilities that he wasn't watching over my shoulder to see what I saw.

"Use my passcode," he said. "If the system undergoes a monitoring check, it won't raise a red flag if official credentials were used to login."

Something that Vaan said felt off. I felt it more than I thought it, a tingling sensation like spiders, real spiders, crawling over my skin in thousands. This wasn't the time to radiate a brighter color or indicate in any other manner that something wasn't right.

But something wasn't right.

"What's your password?" I asked. I hovered my fingers over the keyboard. Vaan spoke a sixteen-digit number sequence that unlocked the system.

It would have been the expected thing to do to access his recent files; see what he'd been working on; run a keyword search on Neptune, HAx5, Cosmos Corsair, or Murder Plot. Vaan's willingness to log into his computer told me he wasn't afraid of what I'd find. It was the confidence of an innocent man who knew he had nothing to hide.

I opened the recently deleted files. Vaan was

too calm. Too confident. Being one hundred percent Plunian, Vaan didn't have the emotional human side that I did, which made him harder to read.

What wasn't hard to read was the document in the Recycle Bin. It was the death notice I'd filed when I first tried to implement my plan to have Neptune declared legally dead. It had been filed like I'd wanted. It would have become part of the hourly newsfeed if not for the actions of one Federation Council member who stopped the distribution.

Vaan had been the one to stop my news bulletin. It satisfied my curiosity but wasn't what I needed to learn. If the news bulletin had never been released, I might have written it off as a clerical error. I would have been back on the Moon Unit, folding uniforms, having to trust that a delay in reporting or a more salacious crime had bumped my story down on the list of news. I might never have known what had happened.

But it wasn't that my story didn't run. It was that another story ran in its place. A murder. Of a prisoner, by a prisoner. The kind of story that would force an internal audit of the Federation Council prison, or at least the illusion of one.

Possibly lead to prison reform if the external world was incensed enough. But would the external world care about the murder of an evil space pirate? Nope. They'd cheer. One less bully in the world.

I glanced up at Vaan and forced a smile. He smiled back. "Thanks," I said. "The system is sluggish. I'm almost in."

"Take your time." He turned his back on me, and I caught his reflection in the frame of the travel poster for Plunia that hung on the wall opposite his desk. He might have become a member of the council, but he hadn't forgotten where he came from. I watched him bend down and pick up the bin of trash and carry it to a chute in the wall. Something about the bin's contents struck me.

"Can you come look at this?" I said. Vaan stopped and turned his head. He seemed conflicted for a moment but only a moment, and then he nodded and walked behind the desk. I closed the recently deleted files and opened the SPIDERs' firewall, eleven down, number twelve firmly in place like it had been when I left Phobos. "I'm up against a firewall. You're a better hacker than I am. Any suggestions?"

"Let me try."

I stood and let Vaan take his seat. He set the trash can down and joined me at the computer. I handed him the blue-light glasses. He put the glasses on, assessed the screen, and started typing. He didn't know what information was hidden behind those six firewalls, and I wasn't about to tell him.

I gave him the same courtesy he gave me and walked away from the desk. I pretended to study the travel poster of Plunia, an unimportant act that I hoped Vaan would dismiss as nostalgia. I propped my left foot on the edge of the trash can and cuffed the hem of my oversize prisoner uniform while looking inside. It seemed an odd time for Vaan to decide to empty his trash, and now I knew why.

30: DARK REFLECTIONS

THE TRASH HELD A PRISONER UNIFORM LIKE the one I wore.

At Space Academy, we learned to add up a series of facts to reach a conclusion. It often wasn't one big piece of information that indicated a truth or a lie but a buildup of small ones that pointed at one inevitable thing. In this case, the little facts built up to one big thing: Vaan was the murderer.

Fact: Vaan had received and killed my news bulletin.

Fact: Vaan was in the prison when the murder had taken place.

Fact: Vaan had a prisoner uniform in his office. *In his trash.*

And what had he told me? Conversations in his

office were recorded. That was his excuse for lying to me the morning I came here, the morning the crime had been committed. But if that were true, then why didn't he care about that now?

Because he knew this time I wouldn't live to tell.

The anxiety I felt earlier returned tenfold. Everything I knew fell into place. With the infrared cameras on and Vaan in a prisoner uniform, he could have gotten away with murder and framed Neptune. The surveillance would have supported that. There was only one problem for Vaan. The witness.

With extreme control, I lowered my foot and looked up at the poster again. Vaan's reflection stared back at me. He wasn't looking at the screen. He was watching me. I couldn't see his eyes thanks to the screen reflecting back off the blue-light glasses—

And I knew why Vaan had given me the courtesy of watching me from in front of the desk. In the reflection of the glasses, I could see his screen. Which meant he had seen mine.

He'd seen me access the Recycle Bin. He knew I knew he was the one behind everything.

"You did it. You killed Cosmos Corsair and

framed Neptune. It had to be you. You were gone from your office when the crime was committed, and you had the ability to delete my news bulletin and replace it with the one that ran." He sat back from the computer and studied me. He didn't deny my charges. "Why, Vaan? After all this time. After losing everything we had. Why risk your career and your future to frame Neptune for murder?"

When he spoke, it was a calm, detached voice. "You surprised me, Sylvia. You let four months go by without even requesting visitation privileges to see Neptune."

"What are you talking about?"

He ignored my question. "At first, that made me happy. I thought you were getting over him. I thought you were moving on. But then I got contacted by a former warden who noticed some unusual search activity on an old interview."

"That's not possible," I said. But it was possible. The day I accessed the interview from the former warden was the day I started to plan. I read that interview a hundred times that night. That interview set this whole thing into motion.

"Oh, but it is possible. Quite. The warden thought it was nothing at first, but protocol obligates him to notify the prison with his findings.

It's a good thing I intercepted that call. Otherwise, you might be serving time inside the jail yourself."

"Like you should be?"

"I saved your life, Sylvia. I expected you to be grateful."

"No," I said. "You didn't commit murder for me. I don't accept that."

"I did, and I'd do it again. Your mission may be to protect the galaxy, but that isn't mine. The galaxy is filled with corruption and scandal, with cheating and lying and evil space pirates."

"But the Federation Council is supposed to protect us. You're one of them. The whole point of a governing body is to regulate the evil and protect the populace."

Vaan stood up from the computer. "Killing Cosmos Corsair did that."

"But Neptune? Why did he have to get pulled into your plan?"

"I'm a peace officer, Sylvia. Acts of violence are verboten in Federation Council. But I've watched Neptune act like he's above the law, and I've watched you fall in love with him. He's as bad as the pirates, don't you see? He takes what he wants with no regard for the rules. He's a threat to our system of structure and law. Until we can control people like him, we can't expect to keep the galaxy safe."

"The whole point of space travel is the freedom," I said. "That's why cruise lines like Moon Unit are successful. People are curious. They want to explore strange new worlds. Seek out new civilizations."

"People aren't as bold or curious as you give them credit for, Sylvia. When's the last time someone surprised you? Acted in a way you never saw coming? When's the last time *your* intellectual curiosity was tested?"

If he meant it as a rhetorical question, a distraction, a redirection of logic that provided some sort of misguided explanation for why he'd done what he'd done, he failed. Because I knew exactly when the last time my intellectual curiosity was tested.

The day I met Neptune.

"Vaan Marshall killed Cosmos Corsair," I shouted to the room. I didn't know where the recording devices was hidden but I was determined to get my accusations on record (even if I didn't survive.) "Vaan Marshall framed Neptune for the murder. Vaan Marshall used his standing as a Federation Council member to cover up his crime."

"Sylvia, don't!" Vaan knocked the computer off his desk and climbed over it. He clamped his hand on my wrist and held tight. I knew twenty defensive maneuvers that had a high probability of freeing me from his grip, but I didn't fight him. He turned me around so my back was up against his, and his elbow was bent by my neck, cutting off my air supply. In the reflection of the travel poster frame, I saw two faces that had once been friends, classmates, and lovers. One deep purple. One magenta.

Magenta? Oh no!

The tingling started a moment later, followed by the sensation of insects stinging me from inside my body. Sparkles spread over my skin like an invisible wand was coating me in glitter paint. And then the center of my hands, arms, legs, and torso glowed a white so bright I wished I were wearing the blue-light glasses. I squeezed my eyes shut and braced myself to be dematerialized into microscopic particles of energy.

31: REMATERIALIZED

"What's your name?" Doc Edison said, shining a bright pencil light into my pupil.

"Get away from me!" I kicked my heels against the floor to push myself away from him.

"Stryker."

"Neptune?"

"Darn it, you big ape! She's supposed to tell me her name, not you." Doc clicked off his penlight. "The girl went through an unexpected dematerialization. Give me five minutes to conduct a physical to make sure she's got her wits about her, and then you can debrief her."

"I can't trust you," I said to Doc.

"Yes, you can," said yet another voice. It was Zeke. I didn't know how he was there, how I was there, or who else was there. "Remember I sent the data breach to Doc's computer?" Zeke continued, as if being on the Moon Unit was the most normal thing in the world. "He noticed something was eating up the available memory in his system. He got Neptune to check it out."

I looked back and forth at Doc and Neptune. "How? Neptune was supposed to be in the holding cell in the subbasement."

The body on the bed next to me shifted. The covers were thrown back, and Ofra sat up. His piercings had been removed and his face was clean of the metallic colors he favored. "Lt. Stryker, I do believe I found a way to remove myself from your debt." He raised his eyebrows at Doc. "It appears my decoy duties are over. Am I free to return to my station?"

Doc waved his hand back and forth. "Go back to Engineering. Captain Major Tom has had his hands full with ground control, and I'm sure he wants to return to the bridge."

Ofra stood. He pulled off the prison uniform, revealing his custom-fitted, spangled, and stretched Moon Unit uniform underneath. He reached into a pocket and pulled out a compact, quickly applying a coat of cobalt-blue metallic eyeshadow. "Ah, to be myself again." He pushed Doc and Zeke out of the way and left Medi-Bay with a spring in his step.

I turned back to Doc. "You and Neptune went through the data breach? What did you find?"

"I found out that you copied classified medical files and sent them to Zeke."

"Yeah, um, sorry about that."

"I also found everything I need to create an antidote to the HAx5 epidemic, and coordinates for the labs that have been synthesizing the drug," Doc said.

"You can shut down Corsair's production?" I asked.

"It's already done."

Aside from having said my name, Neptune was silent. He was normally a man of few words, but he'd said a lot the last time we talked. I didn't know if he remembered any of it. I didn't know whether everything he said was the result of a drug interaction or a bait-and-switch plan to distract me from my mission, and I was afraid to ask.

"How did I get here?" I asked. "The dematerializer only works if you have my coordinates, and nobody could have predicted I'd be in a compromising position in Vaan Marshall's office."

"You're not the only sneaky one around here," Doc answered. "That shot I gave you outside the holding cell—the one that calmed you down—included a chemical tracking compound."

"You mean you knew where I was all along?"

"Yes," Doc said.

As I sat there shaking off the residual effects of the materializer, I turned to Zeke. "Were you dematerialized too?"

"Are you kidding? No way. I got Garson and Lita out like you asked and brought them here in my repair pod."

"They're safe?"

"Yep. They're in Engineering with the Space Cowboys waiting to talk to Ofra," Doc said. "Something about living on Pluto?"

"And Vaan?"

"Locked up in the holding cell."

I looked at Neptune again and caught him watching me. I quickly glanced away but then looked back. His stare was direct and gave away nothing.

Without breaking eye contact, I spoke. "I'm Lt. Sylvia Stryker, second lieutenant overseeing uniforms for the Moon Unit corporation. I'm half Plunian and half human and temporarily live in someone else's ranch house on the Kuiper Belt. I'm a part-time sales representative for Century 21 Uniforms, and I have a history of conducting off-book security missions in my spare time."

Neptune's mouth curled into the tiniest of grins. Doc aimed his diagnostic scanner at me and checked the reading. "We should dematerialize you more often. Seems like you're finally telling us the truth."

32: SERIOUS MOONLIGHT

Doc kicked Zeke out of Medi-Bay first. "Go to my room," I told him. "But be careful. Pika might be there, and there's no telling what she got into while I was gone."

Zeke grinned and left. I stayed in Medi-Bay. Doc carried his medical bag to the door that led to his office. "She's all yours," he said to Neptune.

When the door closed behind Doc, I felt my body start to hum. Neptune held out his hand, and when I took it, he pulled me to my feet.

"You could have told me," I said.

Neptune crossed his arms.

"You could have found a way to let me know you were working from the inside. I spent the past four months hatching a plan to bust you out. Did you think I was going to let you rot in jail? For a crime—not that I personally see what we did as a crime, but that's a detail—that I helped commit? We're a team, Neptune. You need to rely on me a little more."

I put my hands on my hips. To anyone watching, we were in a familiar stance. Me: petite, purple, and plucky; looking at Neptune: massive, muscular, and mad.

Neptune spoke. "When your dad agreed to work with us on the mission to Saturn, he made me promise one thing. He knew of the corruption inside Federation Council, and he knew you were at risk because of your past with Vaan. He wanted me to infiltrate the prison system and see for myself whether Vaan could be trusted."

"My dad never trusted Vaan," I said. "Even back when we dated."

It wasn't lost on me that my dad had turned to Neptune to find out if Vaan was on the up and up. I doubted it was lost on Neptune either.

"Stryker, we need to talk about what happened in the subbasement."

"You mean waking up in your underwear? That was a tactical move."

"I'm talking about what I said."

"Oh." Here it came. The cover story to undo the unexpectedly nice things Neptune told me while under the influence of HAx5. I hated the drug, the pirate who'd synthesized and distributed the drug, the pushers and the dealers and whole seamy side of the addiction industry, but the tiniest part of me liked the effect that drug had had on Neptune.

"I had Doc administer a benign chemical into my bloodstream so I would lose consciousness. That would give him a reason to move me to Medi-Bay. He'd been working on an antidote to Corsair's drug, using me as his test subject, but once I got moved out of the prison, he lost his patient."

"Doc said you were injected with a lethal dose of HAx5."

"That was our cover story. The drug he gave me mimics symptoms that could be anything. The guards were supposed to find me outside the cell. Moon Unit protocol states—"

I cut him off and finished his sentence. "—that any passenger appearing to be carrying a contagion be moved immediately to an isolated room in Medi-Bay for testing." I knew the Book of Protocols better than anyone else on the ship. "That was all an act."

"You weren't supposed to be the one to find me. What were you doing down there?"

"Contacting Zeke. I had to get off the ship, and I had to access the dark web from your old computer to establish a comm link."

"You didn't know I was in the holding cell. When you found me, I wasn't on HAx5, but the easiest way to distract you was to seem like I was."

It had all been an act. The simplest explanation. If it had been me, I would have overcomplicated it, added in a few details for color, and been busted on my lie before I finished telling it. Neptune had a way of seeing right through me.

Neptune leaned back against the counter. "You were going to have me declared legally dead? It's not a bad plan. More dramatic than I would have done but unique. What were you going to tell people when I turned out not to be dead? Or did you not consider that?"

"I had that all figured out. You're Neptune's twin brother, Atlas. Or maybe a clone. Somebody in this galaxy has to have figured out clone technology, right? Maybe there's a lab of Neptune clones being held in reserve to unleash on evil space pirates."

"A clone," he said.

"Yep. I could sell the concept if I had to." We both knew I couldn't.

Neptune smiled. A genuine, warm, I-like-you-Stryker smile. I pulled his dog tags out from under my collar. His arched eyebrows dropped down low over his eyes, immediately changing his expression from warm to suspicious.

"Garson gave them to me. He's your witness."

Neptune nodded. "The kid overheard Corsair making arrangements with two of the prison guards to keep up the distribution of HAx5. He told his sister and asked her advice. She went to Vaan. She was an employee. She saw the news. She knew I'd been watching over Garson, and she knew he would have told her if I was guilty. When he told her he saw Vaan commit murder, she knew her brother was never getting out. None of the prisoners were."

"They're out now." I filled Neptune in on the accidental release of the prison holding system, how I'd turned the infrared lights off and seen the locked-up Plunians while the security guards were coming to get me. "There's a chance that some of the inmates I released deserved to be in jail," I said. "Corsair was locked up, and he was a bad guy. I'm not foolish enough to believe letting everybody go was all good."

"If only we knew of an independent outfit who could take up the job of recapturing the bad guys."

I looked up at Neptune. "I suspect the SPIDERs are available," I said. "I can ask Pika to call them."

"What about you?"

"Capturing bad guys seems so, I don't know, pedestrian. I like a little more of a challenge."

"Nothing says challenge like working Moon Unit security."

"You think we can convince Captain Major Tom to terminate the Stardust Cowboys?"

Neptune winked. "I think the odds are in our favor."

———

My bougie room had turned into a crash pad. In my absence, Pika had gotten into all the sugar that Zeke had arranged for Moon Unit Corporation to stock in my room. She was tucked under my gravity blanket, sleeping it off. Her belly was so full it looked like she'd swallowed a watermelon whole.

DIANE VALLERE

Zeke was on the floor surrounded by components of my disassembled computer. (Pika!) He barely acknowledged my return. I hopped into the sanitary cleaning chamber and blasted off the accumulated dirt and anxiety of the past few days.

I pulled on a robe and went to the uniform ward. Privacy at last.

If the Moon Unit Corporation chose to terminate my employment, I wouldn't fight them. I'd spent less time on the ship than ever before. My area of responsibility was a mess of dirty uniforms in bins, unfolded uniforms falling out of the supply closet, and wrinkled uniforms on the pressing station.

I dug past the current inventory to a uniform I'd stashed when I first arrived, hidden on the bottom of the closet. It was from my first trip with the company. I tossed my robe and put the old uniform on. It wasn't a tech fabric or prototype design, but a pullover uniform that zipped up the back and displayed the Moon Unit Logo in the front.

I spent the next couple of hours doing my job. I repacked the closet, sorted the laundry, and initiated the cleaning sequence, then finally turned off the lights and left. It was the middle of the night. The passengers and crew were probably asleep. It was quiet and calm, and there was only one place I wanted to be. I took the High Velocity Transport System to the observation deck and stared out into the dark, mysterious sky, lit only by traces of moonlight.

I'd believed that there were good forces out there using their wits and skills and moral codes to fight injustice, and that was exactly what I'd found. The SPIDERs. Three Martians who'd taken over an uninhabited moon and built a base from which to work. I wondered if they were the only ones. Or were there others, clusters of good guys fighting the bad, developing and using skills I couldn't begin to imagine? Until now, I'd thought my education at Space Academy was enough to prepare me for the security sector. Now, I knew it was the tip of the iceberg.

The good in the galaxy wasn't the governing body. It was the grass-roots effort. The unregulated do-gooders who fought for freedom because that was what mattered. The SPIDERs had a file filled with evidence to indict Vaan on the charges of murder, but catching a murderer wasn't their end goal. They'd wanted to intercept Neptune and give him an off-the-grid life most likely in exchange for his help with their cause.

The doors swished open behind me. "Stryker," Neptune said. His eyes swept over me. "That's not a regulation uniform."

"It was," I said. "Once."

"Moon Unit 5."

"You remembered."

He walked around the perimeter of the observation deck and stood next to me. My hands were on the banister, and he put his there, too, barely touching mine.

He wore the black security gear he always wore, fitted to show off his broad shoulders and muscular build. It was like Neptune's arrest, my plan to have him declared dead, his hiding out on a Moon Unit, and me being blown apart and put back together all led to this moment, this do-over, where fighting bad guys in outer space was the secondary agenda. I put my hand on top of his and looked up at him. My bright lavender coloring cast a familiar glow. There was no trying to hide my thoughts.

The doors behind us swished open, and Angie Anderson stormed in. Her hair stuck out every which way, her fists were balled up, and her face was twisted in anger.

"Where have you been?" she demanded. "I've wasted the last two hours trying to find you." She glanced at my body. "And why are you always wearing someone else's garments? Are you embarrassed by my designs?"

"Angie, I don't think I'm cut out to be your sales rep," I said.

She continued as if she hadn't heard me. "You've been out of range, out of leads, and now out of uniform. Consider yourself fired. I'll expect my space pod to be returned by morning."

I didn't tell her it was parked at Neptune's ranch.

I didn't tell that I'd spent very little of the past twenty-four hours on sales calls.

I didn't tell her I'd completed a highly dangerous and effective mission to team up with outcast Martians to manage a prison break and expose corruption in Federation Council.

I didn't fight for my job, because I didn't want that job. What I wanted, what I needed, was right here on the Moon Unit. Nothing else mattered.

After Angie left, Neptune bent his head down and kissed me. I kissed him back. And in the privacy of the observation deck, two non-Century 21, non-prototype, no-bells-and-whistles uniforms were discarded in a pile on the floor, and for possibly the first time in both of our lives, Neptune and I each set aside the need to do battle.

And Neptune proved that despite the incarceration, the overdose, the handcuffs and shackles, and everything else that had happened over the past four months, he was very much alive.

(Twice.)

ACKNOWLEDGMENTS

Thank you to Valerie Cassidy for suggesting the name Cosmos Corsair for a space pirate, Red Adept Editing, and David Bowie, for inspiring the title of this book.

ABOUT THE AUTHOR

National bestselling author Diane Vallere writes funny and fashionable character-based mysteries. After two decades working for a top luxury retailer, she traded fashion accessories for accessories to murder in *Designer Dirty Laundry*, her first book. A past president of Sisters in Crime, Diane started her own detective agency at age ten and has maintained a passion for shoes, clues, and clothes ever since.

(The space stuff came when she turned eleven.)

ALSO BY

Samantha Kidd Mysteries

Designer Dirty Laundry

Buyer, Beware

The Brim Reaper

Some Like It Haute

Grand Theft Retro

Pearls Gone Wild

Cement Stilettos

Panty Raid

Union Jacked

Slay Ride

Tough Luxe

Fahrenheit 501

Madison Night Mad for Mod Mysteries

"Midnight Ice" Novella

Pillow Stalk

That Touch of Ink

With Vics You Get Eggroll

The Decorator Who Knew Too Much

The Pajama Frame

Lover Come Hack

Apprehend Me No Flowers

Teacher's Threat

The Kill of it All

Sylvia Stryker Outer Space Mysteries

Fly Me To The Moon

I'm Your Venus

Saturn Night Fever

Spiders from Mars

Material Witness Mysteries

Suede to Rest

Crushed Velvet

Silk Stalkings

Costume Shop Mystery Series

A Disguise to Die For

Masking for Trouble

Dressed to Confess

Mermaid Mysteries

Tails from the Deep

Murky Waters

Sleeping with the Fishes

Non-Fiction

Bonbons For Your Brain

Made in the USA
Las Vegas, NV
23 July 2021

26929889R00173